Book : 1

Ending the New:

Ascension Day

Author/Publisher: B. A. Harris Publishing's

Narrated by:

To my amazing Family, Friends and Medical Team,

Thank you for being there for me in my darkest hour. If not for you all,
I would not be here.

Disclaimer

This book is a fictional interpretation of biblical events and themes as presented in the King James Version (KJV) Bible. The views, opinions, and interpretations expressed in this work are those of the author and do not necessarily reflect the views of any religious institution or organization. The characters, events, and dialogues in this book are purely fictional and are not intended to represent real persons, living or dead, unless explicitly stated otherwise. Any resemblance to actual events or persons, living or dead, is entirely coincidental.

The views and opinions expressed in this book are those of the author and do not necessarily reflect the official policy or position of any distributor, manufacturer, or affiliated organization. The content is intended for informational and entertainment purposes only. The publisher, B. A. Harris Publishing's, and the author accept no responsibility for any errors or omissions, or for any consequences resulting from the use of the information contained in this book.

The views and opinions expressed in the content published by B. A. Harris Publishing's, including books, cartoons, comic books, video games, mobile games, music, art, and poetry, are those of the individual creators and do not necessarily reflect the official policy or position of B. A. Harris Publishing's or any of its affiliates. All content is provided "as is" without warranty of any kind, either express or implied, including but not limited to the implied warranties of merchantability, fitness for a particular purpose, or non-infringement.

B. A. Harris Publishing's is not responsible for any errors or omissions, or for the results obtained from the use of this information. Any action you take upon the information found in the content published by B. A. Harris Publishing's is strictly at your own risk, and B. A. Harris Publishing's will not be liable for any losses or damages in connection with the use of our content.

Distributors

The opinions expressed in this book are solely those of the author and are not endorsed or affiliated with any distributors or manufacturers.

Table of Contents

Prologue: The Prophecy

The world's breath held in a rare, uneasy stillness as dusk fell. Shadows lengthened across the globe, and the once familiar evening news broadcasts now carried a chilling urgency. Anchors, their faces pale and drawn, reported an escalating series of phenomena that defied explanation. The screen flickered with images of vanished families, inexplicable phenomena, and rising global unrest. Panic spread like wildfire, as millions vanished in the blink of an eye.

In a dimly lit study cluttered with ancient texts, Professor Aaron Harris , a renowned biblical scholar, pored over manuscripts illuminated only by the flickering light of a single lamp. His fingers trembled as they traced the worn pages of an ancient Bible. The prophecies of old, which had long been relegated to obscurity, now seemed to come alive with disturbing clarity.

The Book of Revelation, once a distant echo of a bygone era, spoke with a new and foreboding voice: "Behold, I come as a thief in the night; blessed is he that watcheth, and keepeth his garments." Professor Harris's eyes widened with a mix of fear and recognition. The Rapture—a term once relegated to theological debates and esoteric study—was now manifesting in the reality before him.

Across the world, a sense of dread had taken root. Reports of natural disasters—earthquakes, storms, and floods—converged with alarming regularity, creating an apocalyptic tableau. The seas roared, cities crumbled, and the sky itself seemed to darken, reflecting humanity's collective anxiety. The words of the ancient prophecy were no longer distant warnings but immediate, terrifying truths.

As the chaos unfolded, voices of reason and disbelief clashed. Some saw these events as the beginning of the end times, while others scrambled for scientific explanations. In the midst of this turmoil, the ancient prophecies served as a grim reminder of what was foretold—a day when the world would be tested beyond its limits.

Professor Harris's heart pounded as he read the chilling verses that spoke of a time of tribulation and upheaval. The once-clear line between the prophetic and the present had blurred, leaving humanity on the precipice of an era defined by turmoil and divine reckoning. The prophecy had begun, and the world stood on the edge of an abyss, awaiting the full unfolding of the Rapture's portentous promise.

THE STILLNESS OF THE night was pierced by the distant wail of sirens and the murmur of frightened voices. Across the globe, people gathered around their televisions, glued to the screens as the nightmare unfolded. The familiar patterns of everyday life had been shattered, replaced by a chaotic scramble for answers and a desperate search for loved ones who had vanished without a trace.

Professor Aaron Harris looked up from his ancient texts, his mind racing. The prophecies he had studied for years were now playing out in real-time, their ominous warnings coming to life with terrifying precision. He flipped through pages that spoke of the "Great Tribulation" and the "Day of the Lord," his breath quickening as he read passages describing a world in upheaval, divine judgment, and the rise of a powerful, malevolent figure—the Antichrist.

The TV in the corner of his study droned on with news updates, each report more harrowing than the last. Governments around the world were declaring states of emergency, but their efforts to control the situation seemed futile against the sheer scale of the disaster. The media, struggling to keep up, broadcasted images of empty streets, abandoned cars, and the terrified faces of those left behind. Reports of strange phenomena—rivers turning blood-red, stars falling from the sky—added to the growing sense of dread.

As Professor Harris continued his research, he encountered an old, leather-bound book that seemed to resonate with an eerie significance. The title, "The Final Revelation," was embossed in gold letters that gleamed faintly in the dim light. Opening it, he found passages that spoke of celestial signs and the end of days, aligning almost perfectly with the events now unfolding. The words seemed to leap off the pages, almost as if they were meant to be read in this exact moment.

The scholar's mind was a whirlwind of fear and realization. He knew that the coming days would challenge the very essence of human belief and endurance. The prophecy spoke not only of destruction but also of a glimmer of hope—a remnant that would endure through faith and perseverance. Yet, this hope seemed distant as the world spiraled into chaos.

As the night wore on, Professor Harris made a solemn vow. He would not let the fear of the unknown paralyze him. Instead, he resolved to decipher the ancient texts and understand their meaning in the context of the current crisis. The survival of his faith, and perhaps of humanity itself, depended on uncovering the truth behind the prophecy and preparing for the trials that lay ahead.

Outside, the world continued to change irrevocably. The night was alive with the echoes of an age-old prophecy coming to fruition, and as the dawn approached, it brought with it the promise of a new era—one that would test every soul and challenge the very foundations of human belief. Professor Harris knew that this was just the beginning, and the journey ahead would be fraught with peril and revelation.

As the hours crept into the early morning, the sky outside Professor Harris's study began to show the faintest hint of dawn. The first light of day seemed hesitant, as if it, too, feared what lay ahead. Professor Harris continued to pore over his books, driven by a sense of urgency that bordered on desperation. The ancient prophecies, once mere theoretical study, now felt like a blueprint for the tumultuous days ahead.

The prophecy had spoken of a time when "the stars would fall from the sky, and the earth would tremble in its foundations." Across the globe, reports of celestial phenomena—mysterious flashes, shifting constellations, and the eerie, sudden darkness of the day—seemed to fulfill these ominous predictions. Scientists and astronomers struggled to provide explanations, but their efforts were overshadowed by the sheer scale of the disruptions.

In the midst of this turmoil, a figure emerged in the media—an enigmatic man who claimed to have answers. He spoke with an almost magnetic charisma, offering a mixture of comfort and cryptic warnings. This man, whom some had begun to call the "Charismatic Leader," seemed to have an uncanny grasp of the situation. His speeches were filled with references to ancient prophecies, and he presented himself as a beacon of hope in a world shrouded in confusion.

Professor Harris watched these broadcasts with growing concern. There was something unsettling about this figure's rise to prominence. His promises of salvation were seductive, but his demeanor and the fervor with which he spoke of a new world order carried an undercurrent of manipulation. As the scholar analyzed the texts, he found troubling parallels between the leader's rhetoric and the descriptions of the Antichrist in the prophecies.

Determined to make sense of it all, Professor Harris reached out to colleagues and fellow scholars, trying to piece together the fragments of a shattered world. The communications were fraught with difficulty, as the global infrastructure was under severe strain. Many scholars, once thought to be reliable, were now missing or unresponsive. The uncertainty of their situation made it clear that the world was on the brink of an unprecedented transformation.

In his solitary vigil, Professor Harris found a disturbing revelation within the ancient texts—an account of a time when humanity would face its greatest trial, a period marked by intense suffering and moral testing. This trial would reveal the true nature of humanity and the strength of its faith. As the prophecy foretold, it was not merely a time of destruction but a profound test of spiritual endurance and resolve.

As dawn broke and the first light of morning pierced the gloom, Professor Harris looked out of his window, reflecting on the dark horizon. The world was changing rapidly, and the ancient prophecies seemed to be unfolding with a chilling precision. The once-clear line between divine prophecy and present reality had vanished, leaving humanity to navigate an uncertain future.

In this moment of dawning clarity, Professor Harris knew that the time for reflection and study was over. The prophecy had begun, and the coming days would demand more than academic knowledge. They would require courage, faith, and an unwavering commitment to uncovering the truth.

With a heavy heart but a resolute spirit, Professor Harris prepared to embark on a journey that would test not only his intellect but also his faith. The prophecy had cast its shadow over the world, and as the dawn of a new era approached, humanity stood at the threshold of its greatest trial—a trial that would define the course of history and the fate of every soul.

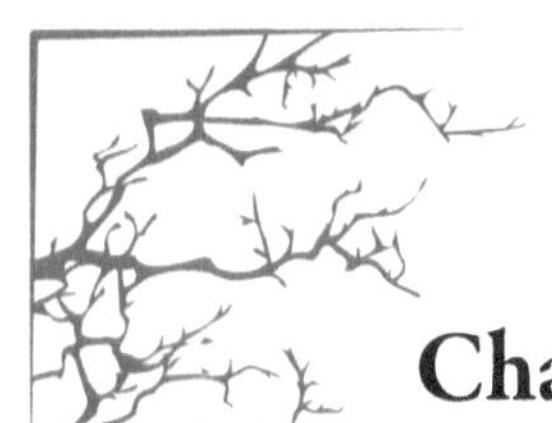

Chapter 1: The Unraveling

JOHN CARTER'S MORNING routine was as ordinary as any other. The sun had just begun to rise, casting a warm, golden light through the kitchen window of his suburban home. He sipped his coffee, a moment of calm before the rush of the day. His wife, Emily, prepared breakfast while their children, Sarah and David, chatted animatedly about their plans for the day. The routine felt comforting, a semblance of normalcy in a world that had always been predictable.

The peace of the morning, however, was abruptly shattered by the blaring news alerts on the television. The screen displayed a series of flashing headlines and breaking news updates that painted a picture of widespread chaos. John's attention was drawn away from his newspaper as the anchor's grave voice filled the room.

"...Reports are coming in from around the world of inexplicable disappearances. Thousands of people have vanished without a trace in the last 24 hours. Authorities are scrambling to understand the cause..."

Emily's face paled as she looked at the screen, her hands pausing mid-air as she tried to process the gravity of the news. John's brow furrowed, a knot of concern tightening in his chest. The children, initially excited about their day, grew quiet as the severity of the situation sank in.

John turned to Emily, his voice steady but tinged with worry. "We need to check on our neighbors and make sure everyone's okay. This doesn't look like a simple technical glitch or an isolated incident."

They quickly dressed and left the house, their neighborhood unusually silent for a Monday morning. The usual sounds of children playing and cars passing by were replaced with an eerie stillness. As they walked down the street, they noticed other families doing the same—searching, calling out, and trying to make sense of the inexplicable.

At the local community center, which had become an impromptu gathering spot, confusion and fear reigned. People huddled in small groups, exchanging stories of loved ones who had disappeared. The sense of solidarity among the neighbors was palpable, but so was the underlying anxiety. The center's director, a man named Mr. Jenkins, stood at the podium, his voice trembling as he addressed the crowd.

"We don't know much yet, but we're doing everything we can to find out what's happening. Please, stay in contact with your loved ones and report any missing persons immediately."

John and Emily spoke with Mr. Jenkins, who could only offer a helpless shrug in response to their questions. They returned home with a growing sense of dread. The television continued to broadcast images of empty streets, abandoned vehicles, and distraught families. News reports suggested that the phenomenon was global in scope, affecting people of all ages and backgrounds.

As the day wore on, the initial shock began to give way to a more profound unease. John and Emily tried to maintain a sense of normalcy for their children, but it was clear that their world had irrevocably changed. The very fabric of their daily lives had been torn apart, leaving them grappling with an uncertain future.

In the evening, as darkness settled over the neighborhood, the power flickered and went out, plunging the house into an unsettling quiet. John, trying to comfort his family, found solace in the small, flickering candlelight. They gathered together, sharing stories and memories to distract from the growing sense of fear and loss.

The next morning brought no relief. The global news was even graver, with reports of widespread infrastructure failures, panic buying, and a breakdown of public order. Governments around the world declared states of emergency, but their efforts seemed insufficient against the scale of the crisis. The Carter family, like millions of others, was left to navigate a new reality where the rules of the old world no longer applied.

John sat by the window, staring out at the neighborhood, which now felt like a ghost town. The once-familiar streets seemed alien and foreboding. He held Emily's hand tightly, a silent promise to face the unknown together. The world had unraveled overnight, and the future was a dark, uncharted territory.

As the days stretched on, John realized that the disappearance of millions was only the beginning. The echoes of ancient prophecies and the tremors of impending events loomed large. The world had changed in ways they were only beginning to comprehend, and the Carter family stood on the precipice of a new, uncertain era.

The days following the initial chaos were marked by a growing sense of disorientation and desperation. For John Carter, the initial shock had given way to a gnawing anxiety that clung to him like a shadow. The neighborhood that had once been bustling with life now felt eerily deserted, as if a veil had descended, obscuring the familiar and revealing a world transformed.

The Carter family's attempts to reestablish some semblance of routine were thwarted by the continued disruptions. The power outages persisted, and with them, the breakdown of communication systems. Phone lines and internet connections were sporadic, making it difficult to get any reliable information about what was happening beyond their immediate surroundings.

John and Emily spent their days trying to maintain order and provide a sense of normalcy for Sarah and David. They rationed their supplies carefully, knowing that the scarcity of essentials was becoming a growing concern. Emily, who had always been the heart of their home, took on the role of calm caretaker, but her eyes betrayed her anxiety. John, in turn, focused on finding ways to stay informed and keep his family safe.

One evening, John ventured out to the local supermarket to stock up on supplies. What had once been a routine errand turned into a sobering experience. The store, normally bustling with shoppers, was now a scene of disorder. Shelves were empty, and the few remaining patrons were frantically grabbing what they could. The store's manager, a harried woman named Lisa, stood by the entrance, trying to maintain some sense of order.

"John," she said, her voice strained. "I've never seen anything like this. It's not just here; it's everywhere. We're getting reports that entire cities are in chaos."

John nodded, his mind racing with the implications. "Have you heard anything from the authorities? Any idea what's causing this?"

Lisa shook her head. "No clear answers. The government's message is fragmented. Some say it's a massive technical failure, others are talking about some kind of global event. But the more I hear, the less it makes sense."

John returned home with what he could carry, feeling a deep sense of helplessness. The struggle to make sense of the situation seemed to grow with each passing hour. He and Emily spent their evenings discussing their options, trying to plan for a future that seemed increasingly uncertain.

One night, as they sat around the dinner table, their conversation was interrupted by a loud, urgent knock on the door. John opened it to find a neighbor, Tom Williams, standing outside with a worried expression.

"John, I need your help," Tom said. "My wife, Janet, and I, we're trying to find our son. He's missing, and we can't get any information. Have you heard anything about the disappearances? Do you know where we can look for answers?"

John's heart sank at the sight of Tom's distress. "I'm so sorry, Tom. We're all in the same boat here. I wish I had answers. But if you want, we can search together. Maybe there's something we're missing."

The two men set out into the night, their flashlights cutting through the darkness. The streets, once familiar and safe, now felt foreign and menacing. They combed through the neighborhood, calling out for Tom's son, but the silence was unyielding.

As they walked, they noticed other search parties—families and friends, all united by their fear and uncertainty. The sense of community was palpable, but it was overshadowed by a shared sense of dread. The disappearance of millions had left a void that seemed to swallow any hope or assurance.

By the time they returned home, it was well past midnight. Exhausted but resolute, John and Tom parted ways, each carrying the weight of their personal fears. John returned to his family, trying to offer comfort despite the growing realization that their world had irrevocably changed.

As John lay in bed that night, his thoughts were a tumultuous mix of anxiety and determination. The disappearance of millions was not just a physical loss but a profound disruption of their reality. The world they knew was unraveling, and the new reality was as uncertain as it was frightening.

In the darkness, John resolved to seek out answers, not just for himself and his family but for everyone grappling with the same fear and confusion. The prophesied events seemed to be unfolding before their eyes, and the future promised to be a journey fraught with peril and discovery.

The dawn of the next day brought with it no clear answers, but John knew that he could no longer remain passive. The events of the past few days had set in motion a series of events that would challenge his faith, his resolve, and his understanding of the world. As he prepared to face the day, he felt a growing sense of urgency to uncover the truth behind the unfolding prophecy and to navigate the treacherous path that lay ahead.

The days continued to blur together as John and his family struggled to adapt to their new reality. The sense of unease that had settled over their home had not lessened; if anything, it had deepened, becoming a constant, oppressive presence. The disappearance of millions had left a void not just in the physical world but in the hearts and minds of those who remained.

On the third day after the strange occurrences began, John decided to visit the church. It was a Sunday, and under normal circumstances, the church would have been filled with the faithful, gathered to worship and seek solace in their shared beliefs. But as John approached the building, he saw that it was nearly deserted. The sight was a jarring contrast to the usual bustling scene, and it filled him with a deep sense of loss.

He pushed open the heavy wooden doors and stepped inside. The interior of the church was dimly lit, the only light coming from a few flickering candles placed near the altar. A handful of people were scattered throughout the pews, their heads bowed in prayer. The air was thick with an unspoken grief, a collective mourning for the loved ones who had vanished.

At the front of the church, Pastor Williams stood by the pulpit, his hands resting on the open Bible before him. His face was etched with worry, his usual calm demeanor replaced by a visible tension. John walked quietly down the aisle and took a seat in one of the pews near the front. He watched as the pastor slowly raised his head and addressed the small congregation.

"My dear brothers and sisters," Pastor Williams began, his voice trembling slightly. "We are living through a time of great trial. The events of the past few days have shaken us to our core, and we are left searching for answers that seem beyond our grasp. I know that many of you are frightened, confused, and grieving for those who have disappeared. I share your pain, and I stand with you in our search for understanding."

He paused, his gaze sweeping over the congregation. "The Bible tells us in 1 Thessalonians 4:16-17, 'For the Lord himself shall descend from heaven with a shout, with the voice of the archangel, and with the trump of God: and the dead in Christ shall rise first: Then we which are alive and remain shall be caught up together with them in the clouds, to meet the Lord in the air: and so shall we ever be with the Lord.' These words have been a source of comfort for believers throughout the ages, a promise of hope for the faithful."

"But now," he continued, his voice growing more intense, "we must ask ourselves: Is this the time? Are we witnessing the fulfillment of prophecy? Is this the Rapture foretold in Scripture, the moment when the faithful are taken up to be with the Lord?"

The question hung in the air, heavy with the weight of uncertainty. John felt a chill run down his spine as he considered the possibility. Was it true? Had the Rapture begun, leaving those who remained to face the tribulation that was to follow?

Pastor Williams closed his eyes and bowed his head in prayer. "Heavenly Father," he prayed, "we come before You in our hour of need, seeking Your guidance and wisdom. Help us to understand the events unfolding around us. Give us the strength to endure the trials that lie ahead, and the faith to trust in Your divine plan. We ask this in the name of Your Son, our Savior, Jesus Christ. Amen."

The small congregation murmured their own amen, their voices blending together in a soft chorus of supplication. John closed his eyes and joined them in prayer, his mind racing with thoughts of what might come next. He prayed for his family, for their safety and their faith, and for the strength to face whatever challenges lay ahead.

After the service, John approached Pastor Williams, who was standing near the altar, speaking quietly with a few other parishioners. When the pastor saw John, he excused himself and walked over to him.

"John," Pastor Williams said, extending his hand, "I'm glad to see you here today. How are you holding up?"

John shook the pastor's hand and offered a weary smile. "We're doing our best, Pastor, but it's been tough. The kids are scared, and Emily and I are trying to keep things together. But I have to admit, I'm struggling to make sense of all this."

The pastor nodded, his expression sympathetic. "I understand, John. None of us were prepared for something like this. I've been spending a lot of time in prayer, asking for guidance. The Scriptures tell us that these things must come to pass, but it's difficult to face them when they're happening before our eyes."

"Do you really think this could be the Rapture?" John asked, his voice tinged with a mixture of fear and hope.

Pastor Williams sighed deeply. "I wish I could give you a definitive answer, John. The signs are certainly there, and the sudden disappearances are hard to explain by any other means. But whether this is truly the Rapture or not, one thing is clear: we need to be vigilant and prepared. Our faith will be tested in the days ahead, and we must remain strong in our trust in God's plan."

John nodded, absorbing the pastor's words. "Thank you, Pastor. I'll do my best to keep my family grounded in faith. I just hope we can find some answers soon."

The pastor placed a reassuring hand on John's shoulder. "You're not alone in this, John. We will face this together, as a community of believers. Lean on each other, support one another, and above all, keep praying. God will guide us through these troubled times."

John left the church feeling a little more centered, though the uncertainty still gnawed at him. As he walked back to his car, he noticed a group of people gathered near the church steps, engaged in an animated discussion. Curious, he approached them and recognized a few of his neighbors among the group.

One of the men, a stern-faced older gentleman named Harold, was speaking with a tone of authority. "I don't care what anyone says," Harold was saying, "this is the beginning of the end. I've been studying prophecy for years, and I can tell you, this is exactly what the Bible warns us about. We're in the last days, and we'd better get ready."

A younger woman, her voice filled with worry, interjected, "But what are we supposed to do? How do we prepare for something like this?"

Harold looked around at the group, his expression grave. "We pray, we study the Scriptures, and we stay vigilant. The Antichrist will rise, and the tribulation will follow. We need to be ready to stand firm in our faith, no matter what comes."

John listened quietly, feeling a mixture of apprehension and resolve. The conversation confirmed what he had feared: the events unfolding around them were not just random occurrences but part of something much larger and more significant. The world was on the brink of a great tribulation, and there was no turning back.

As he drove home, John's thoughts returned to his family. He needed to protect them, to prepare them for the challenges ahead. The pastor's words echoed in his mind: "Our faith will be tested." John knew that his family's survival would depend not just on physical preparedness but on their spiritual strength as well.

When he arrived home, Emily was waiting for him in the living room, her face lined with worry. "How was the service?" she asked, her voice tentative.

John sat down beside her, taking her hand in his. "It was sobering," he admitted. "Pastor Williams spoke about the possibility that this could be the Rapture. He doesn't know for sure, but the signs are there. He said we need to be prepared, to stay strong in our faith."

Emily nodded, her eyes filling with tears. "I'm scared, John. I don't know what's going to happen, and I hate that our kids have to go through this."

"I know," John said, pulling her into a comforting embrace. "But we're going to get through this together. We have to stay strong, for each other and for the kids. We'll lean on our faith and on each other, and we'll face whatever comes, one day at a time."

As they held each other, John felt a renewed sense of determination. The road ahead was uncertain and fraught with danger, but he knew that his family's strength lay in their unity and their faith. No matter what the future held, they would face it together, anchored in their trust in God and in the love they shared.

And so, as the days continued to unfold with new challenges and revelations, the Carter family braced themselves for the trials that lay ahead, knowing that the prophecy was only just beginning to reveal its full scope. The world around them was unraveling, but within their home, they would fight to hold on to the hope and faith that had always guided them.

As night fell once more, John stood by the window, looking out at the darkened streets. In the distance, he could see the faint glow of fires, the signs of unrest spreading through the city. The air was thick with the tension of a world on the edge of something unprecedented.

But in that moment, as he stood in the quiet of his home, John felt a sense of calm settle over him. The future was uncertain, but he knew where his strength lay. Whatever came next, they would face it together, with faith as their guide and love as their shield.

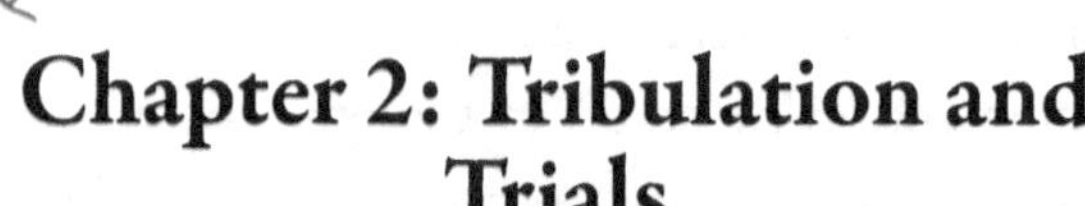

Chapter 2: Tribulation and Trials

THE MORNING LIGHT FILTERED through the curtains, casting a soft glow over the kitchen as Emily prepared breakfast. The familiar sounds of sizzling bacon and the aroma of freshly brewed coffee should have been comforting, but in the days following the disappearances, even the most mundane routines felt surreal. John sat at the table, staring blankly at his plate. His thoughts were far from the breakfast before him; they were consumed by the events of the past week and the uncertainty that lay ahead.

"John, you're not eating," Emily said gently, placing a hand on his shoulder. He looked up at her, offering a faint smile.

"Just thinking," he replied, picking up his fork. "It's hard to focus on anything else."

Emily nodded, her own expression troubled. "I know. But we have to keep going. For the kids."

John glanced over at the children, who were seated at the table, their faces pale and drawn. Lily, their youngest, was pushing her food around on her plate, her usual cheerful chatter replaced by a heavy silence. Matthew, their teenage son, was staring intently at his phone, searching for any news that might provide some answers.

"Anything new?" John asked Matthew, trying to sound hopeful.

Matthew shook his head. "Nothing that makes sense, Dad. Just more reports of chaos... riots, looting, and people panicking. The government keeps saying they're working on it, but they don't know what's going on any more than we do."

John sighed, running a hand through his hair. "We'll just have to stay strong and stick together. We'll figure this out."

As they finished breakfast in silence, the weight of the situation pressed down on them like an invisible force. The world outside their door was changing rapidly, and it was becoming clear that life as they knew it would never be the same.

Later that day, John decided to take a drive around town to see the extent of the damage and to pick up some supplies. Emily insisted on coming with him, leaving the kids with their neighbor, Mrs. Jacobs, who had also lost family members in the disappearances.

As they drove through the streets, the scene that greeted them was one of devastation. Businesses were boarded up, their windows shattered by looters. The once-bustling downtown area was eerily quiet, save for a few people moving about quickly, their eyes darting around with a mix of fear and suspicion. In the distance, they could see smoke rising from what appeared to be another fire, likely set by those who had taken advantage of the chaos.

"This is insane," Emily whispered, gripping John's hand tightly as they passed by a group of armed men standing on a street corner, their faces hard and unyielding.

John nodded, his jaw clenched. "People are scared, and when fear takes over, they do desperate things. We need to be careful."

They reached the grocery store, only to find it nearly empty. Shelves that once held canned goods, bottled water, and other essentials were now barren. A few scattered items remained, but they were quickly being snatched up by frantic shoppers.

John grabbed a cart and moved swiftly through the aisles, picking up what he could find: a few cans of soup, a couple of bags of rice, some dried beans. Emily managed to find some powdered milk and a box of granola bars. It wasn't much, but it would have to do.

As they approached the checkout, they noticed a man arguing with the cashier, his voice rising in anger. "This is all you've got left? How am I supposed to feed my family with this?"

The cashier, a young woman with tired eyes, shrugged helplessly. "I'm sorry, sir. We're doing our best to restock, but deliveries have been delayed. There's nothing more I can do."

The man slammed his fist on the counter, causing the items in his basket to spill onto the floor. "This is unacceptable! We deserve better than this!"

John stepped forward, placing a reassuring hand on the man's shoulder. "Hey, we're all in this together. Let's not make things worse. We're all trying to survive here."

The man turned to John, his eyes wild with desperation. For a moment, it seemed like he might lash out, but then his shoulders slumped, and he sighed heavily. "You're right. I'm sorry. It's just... I don't know how much more of this I can take."

John nodded sympathetically. "None of us do. But we have to stay calm and help each other. That's the only way we're going to get through this."

The man gave a small, reluctant nod before gathering his things and leaving the store. John and Emily paid for their supplies and headed back to the car, the tension from the encounter lingering in the air.

As they drove home, Emily broke the silence. "How long do you think this will last, John? How long before things go back to normal?"

John tightened his grip on the steering wheel, his eyes fixed on the road ahead. "I don't know, Emily. I really don't. But I have a feeling that 'normal' is something we're not going to see for a long time—if ever."

That evening, after the kids had gone to bed, John and Emily sat together on the couch, the flickering light from the television casting shadows on the walls. The news reports were grim: civil unrest was spreading, with reports of violence and looting coming in from cities across the country. The government had declared a state of emergency, but it seemed powerless to stop the chaos.

"John," Emily said softly, breaking the heavy silence, "what are we going to do if this gets worse? How are we going to protect the kids?"

John turned to look at her, his expression resolute. "We'll do whatever it takes. We'll keep them safe, no matter what. But we need to be prepared. Things are already bad, and I have a feeling they're going to get worse before they get better."

Emily nodded, her eyes brimming with tears. "I don't want to lose you, John. I don't want to lose any of us."

He pulled her close, wrapping his arms around her as she buried her face in his chest. "You won't," he whispered fiercely. "I promise you, Emily, we'll get through this. We'll survive."

But even as he said the words, John couldn't shake the feeling that the world was spiraling out of control, and that their survival would depend not just on their determination but on forces beyond their understanding. The prophecy was unfolding, and the tribulation had only just begun.

As the night wore on, John lay awake in bed, staring at the ceiling. The house was quiet, but outside, he could hear distant sirens and the occasional shout. The world was changing, and the comfortable life they had known was slipping away, replaced by a new reality filled with uncertainty, danger, and fear.

In the darkness, John whispered a prayer, asking for strength, guidance, and protection for his family. He knew that the trials they were facing were only the beginning and that they would need every ounce of faith and courage to navigate the treacherous path ahead.

And so, as the first signs of dawn began to creep into the sky, John resolved to be strong for his family, to lead them through the tribulation with unwavering faith. The trials ahead would test them in ways they had never imagined, but they would face them together, armed with their belief in God's plan and their love for one another.

The world around them was descending into chaos, but within the Carter household, there was still hope—hope that they could weather the storm and emerge on the other side, stronger and more united than ever before.

AS THE DAYS PASSED, the world continued to unravel at an alarming pace. The news was a constant stream of chaos and confusion, with reports of entire cities descending into anarchy. Governments around the globe struggled to maintain control, but their efforts seemed increasingly futile. Panic and fear had taken hold, and society was beginning to fracture under the strain.

John and Emily did their best to shield the children from the worst of it, but the reality of their situation was impossible to ignore. The once-friendly neighborhood was now marked by tension and suspicion. Neighbors who had once exchanged pleasantries over garden fences now avoided each other's eyes, distrustful of everyone and everything.

At home, John took on the role of protector with a grim sense of duty. He reinforced the doors and windows, prepared emergency supplies, and kept a watchful eye on the streets. Emily, meanwhile, tried to maintain a sense of normalcy for the children, though it became increasingly difficult with each passing day.

One afternoon, as John was in the garage organizing their supplies, Emily came to him, her face pale and anxious.

"John, we need to talk," she said quietly, glancing over her shoulder to ensure the children weren't within earshot.

John set down the toolbox he was holding and turned to face her. "What's wrong?"

"It's Matthew," she said, her voice trembling. "He's been asking a lot of questions—about the disappearances, about the chaos we're seeing on the news. He's scared, John. And honestly, so am I."

John took a deep breath, wiping his hands on a rag as he considered his response. "I know it's scary, Emily. But we have to stay strong—for them, and for each other. We've got to have faith that we'll get through this."

"I'm trying," Emily said, her eyes filling with tears. "But how do we explain this to the kids? How do we make sense of something that doesn't make any sense at all?"

John reached out and pulled her into an embrace, holding her tightly as she began to cry. "We tell them the truth, Emily. We tell them that we don't have all the answers, but that we trust in God's plan, even if we don't understand it. And we tell them that no matter what happens, we'll face it together."

She nodded against his chest, her tears soaking into his shirt. "I just want them to be safe, John. I want us all to be safe."

"We will be," John murmured, though he couldn't ignore the knot of fear tightening in his own stomach. He kissed the top of her head, then gently pulled back to look her in the eyes. "We'll do whatever it takes to keep them safe."

That evening, John and Emily sat down with the children in the living room. The television was off, and the room was filled with a tense silence as they prepared to have the difficult conversation they had been avoiding.

"Kids," John began, his voice calm but serious, "we need to talk about what's been happening lately. I know you've both noticed that things aren't... normal."

Matthew and Lily looked at their father with wide eyes, both nodding slowly.

Matthew was the first to speak. "Dad, what's going on? Why are all these people disappearing? And why is everyone so scared?"

John exchanged a glance with Emily before turning back to his son. "Matthew, the truth is, we don't know exactly why this is happening. There are a lot of theories out there, but no one has any real answers. What we do know is that the world is going through a very difficult time right now, and things are going to be different for a while."

"Different how?" Lily asked, her small voice trembling with fear.

John sighed, wishing he could offer them more reassurance. "Well, we're going to have to be extra careful. We need to stick together and look out for each other. Things might be hard for a while, but we're going to get through it as a family."

Emily chimed in, her voice soothing. "We need to remember that we're not alone. God is with us, and He has a plan for all of us, even if we don't understand it right now. We have to trust in Him and in each other."

Matthew looked down at his hands, his brow furrowed in thought. "But what if something happens to us? What if we disappear too?"

John felt his heart ache at the fear in his son's voice. He reached over and placed a hand on Matthew's shoulder. "We're going to do everything we can to make sure that doesn't happen, Matthew. We're going to be careful, and we're going to pray for God's protection. But whatever happens, we'll face it together."

Lily crawled into Emily's lap, her eyes wide with worry. "I don't want to disappear, Mommy."

"You're not going to disappear, sweetie," Emily said, hugging her daughter tightly. "We're all going to be right here, taking care of each other."

The family sat together for a long time, holding each other close as they prayed for strength, guidance, and protection. The uncertainty of the future loomed over them like a dark cloud, but in that moment, they found comfort in their shared faith and in the love that bound them together.

In the days that followed, John and Emily worked tirelessly to prepare for whatever might come next. They stocked up on supplies, reinforced their home's defenses, and made plans for different scenarios. John kept a close eye on the news, though the reports only seemed to grow more troubling with each passing day.

As the tribulations mounted, so too did the trials they faced. Power outages became frequent, and with them came the fear of looters and desperate people willing to do anything for food and supplies. The local authorities were overwhelmed, and the streets grew increasingly dangerous.

One evening, as the family sat down to a candlelit dinner during another blackout, they heard a commotion outside—a series of loud bangs, followed by shouting and the sound of breaking glass. John motioned for Emily and the kids to stay quiet, then grabbed the baseball bat he kept by the front door and cautiously peeked out the window.

In the dim light, he could see a group of men outside, ransacking a neighbor's house. They were armed and aggressive, their shouts echoing through the street as they smashed windows and kicked down the door. John's heart raced as he watched them, realizing just how quickly the situation could spiral out of control.

He quickly returned to the kitchen, his face grim. "We need to be ready to leave at a moment's notice. Pack a bag with essentials—clothes, food, water, anything we might need if we have to get out of here fast."

Emily nodded, her expression filled with fear but also determination. She hurried to gather supplies, while John kept watch, praying that the men wouldn't turn their attention toward their house.

The night passed uneventfully, but the encounter left the family on edge. John knew that they couldn't stay in their home indefinitely. The world outside was becoming too dangerous, and they needed to consider finding a safer place—perhaps a remote area where they could wait out the worst of the chaos.

As they discussed their options, the children listened quietly, their young minds struggling to grasp the magnitude of what was happening. John could see the fear in their eyes, and it broke his heart to know that their childhood innocence had been shattered by the events unfolding around them.

But despite the challenges they faced, John was determined to keep his family safe. He knew that the trials ahead would test them in ways they had never imagined, but he also knew that they would face them together, strengthened by their faith and by the love they shared.

And so, with each passing day, they prepared for the unknown, clinging to the hope that they would survive the tribulation and emerge on the other side, ready to rebuild their lives in a world forever changed.

As the chaos continued to spread, the eerie quiet that had settled over the neighborhood began to feel more suffocating. The world outside seemed to be disintegrating, and the Carter family found themselves increasingly isolated. The once-friendly faces of their neighbors had become distant memories as the community fractured under the pressure of fear and uncertainty.

John and Emily spent most of their time strategizing and preparing for the worst. They spoke in hushed tones, discussing escape routes, potential safe havens, and ways to protect their children from the horrors that were becoming all too common. Every night, John took it upon himself to stay awake as long as possible, keeping watch over his family and praying for a sense of normalcy that he feared might never return.

The children, Matthew and Lily, had become uncharacteristically quiet. They clung to their parents, sensing the gravity of the situation even if they didn't fully understand it. The once-familiar routine of their daily lives had been upended, replaced by an uneasy vigilance that pervaded every moment.

It was on the morning of the seventh day since the first disappearances that everything changed. John was in the kitchen, pouring himself a cup of coffee, when the television in the living room blared to life with an emergency broadcast. The sudden noise startled him, and he rushed into the room, nearly spilling his coffee in the process.

Emily was already there, standing frozen in front of the screen, her hand covering her mouth in shock. The children, who had been playing quietly with their toys, looked up at the television, their innocent eyes wide with fear.

On the screen, a news anchor struggled to maintain her composure as she reported on a new wave of disappearances—this one even more widespread and devastating than the last. Entire cities had been left in disarray as millions more people vanished without a trace. The footage that accompanied the report was chaotic: abandoned cars on highways, empty homes with doors left ajar, and streets eerily devoid of life.

"What's happening?" Matthew whispered, his voice trembling.

John didn't have an answer. He stared at the screen, trying to process the magnitude of what he was seeing. This wasn't just a localized event—it was global, affecting every corner of the world. The implications were staggering.

As the broadcast continued, the anchor's voice became increasingly panicked. Reports were coming in of accidents, fires, and other disasters as vehicles crashed and buildings burned, their operators suddenly gone. There were rumors of planes falling from the sky, their pilots having disappeared mid-flight. The images on the screen were horrifying, a stark reminder of how fragile civilization truly was.

"We need to go," John said suddenly, his voice cutting through the shock that had gripped his family. "We can't stay here. It's not safe anymore."

Emily nodded, her eyes filled with tears. She knew he was right, but the thought of leaving their home—the only place that had ever felt truly safe—was almost too much to bear.

"Where will we go?" Lily asked, her small voice breaking John's heart.

"We'll go somewhere safe," John replied, trying to sound reassuring. "Somewhere far away from all of this. We'll be okay, I promise."

They moved quickly, gathering the essentials they had already packed in case they needed to leave in a hurry. John loaded the bags into their car while Emily made sure the children had their most important belongings—a few favorite toys, some clothes, and their Bibles.

As they prepared to leave, John took one last look around their home. The memories of happier times flooded back to him—the laughter, the warmth, the sense of security that had once filled these walls. But now, those memories seemed like distant echoes, overshadowed by the grim reality that had taken hold of their world.

He turned back to his family, who were waiting by the door, and forced a smile. "Let's go."

The drive out of the city was tense and fraught with uncertainty. The streets were a mix of chaos and desolation—some areas were eerily empty, while others were clogged with traffic as panicked residents tried to flee. John kept his eyes on the road, navigating through the confusion while Emily kept the children occupied in the back seat.

As they drove, the radio filled the car with a steady stream of emergency broadcasts and frantic updates. The government was urging people to remain calm and stay indoors, but John knew that staying put wasn't an option. They needed to get away from the densely populated areas, away from the violence and the fear that had gripped the city.

The further they drove, the more isolated the landscape became. The tall buildings of the city gave way to open fields and winding roads, and the sense of urgency began to ebb, replaced by a heavy silence that settled over the car. They were leaving behind everything they had ever known, venturing into the unknown with no clear destination in mind—only the hope of finding safety.

After several hours of driving, John pulled off the highway and onto a narrow road that led into a dense forest. The sun was beginning to set, casting long shadows across the road as they wound their way through the trees. The air was cooler here, and the sense of isolation was palpable.

"We'll stop here for the night," John said, pulling the car into a small clearing. "It's secluded enough that we should be safe until we can figure out our next move."

Emily nodded, though John could see the fear in her eyes. The children, exhausted from the long drive, had fallen asleep in the back seat. They carefully lifted them out of the car and laid them down in the back with blankets, creating a makeshift bed where they could rest.

John and Emily sat together on the hood of the car, watching the last light of day fade into darkness. The quiet of the forest was almost unnerving, a stark contrast to the chaos they had left behind. For the first time in days, there was no sound of sirens, no distant shouts or breaking glass—just the rustling of leaves in the wind and the occasional call of a night bird.

"We can't keep running forever," Emily said softly, breaking the silence. "What are we going to do, John?"

John wrapped an arm around her, pulling her close. "I don't know," he admitted, his voice heavy with uncertainty. "But we'll figure it out. We have to."

They sat in silence for a long time, each lost in their own thoughts. John's mind raced with possibilities—where they could go, how they would survive, what they would do if things continued to deteriorate. But no matter how much he tried to plan, the future remained shrouded in uncertainty.

As the stars began to twinkle overhead, John closed his eyes and said a silent prayer. He prayed for guidance, for strength, and for the safety of his family. He prayed for the world, for those who had disappeared, and for those left behind to make sense of the chaos.

Most of all, he prayed for hope—hope that, despite everything, they would find a way to survive the tribulation that had befallen them. And as he held Emily close, feeling the steady rise and fall of her breath, he clung to that hope with all his might.

The night passed slowly, with John keeping a vigilant watch while Emily and the children slept. Every rustle in the bushes or distant sound in the forest put him on edge, but the night remained uneventful. As dawn began to break, painting the sky in shades of pink and gold, John allowed himself to relax slightly.

They had made it through the night, but he knew the real challenges were yet to come.

Chapter 3: The New Order

THE WORLD HAD BECOME a strange and terrifying place in the wake of the disappearances. The sun still rose and set, but everything else felt different—hollow and surreal, as if the very fabric of reality had been altered. Those who remained were left to grapple with the unimaginable loss of loved ones and the unsettling feeling that nothing would ever be the same again.

For John Carter and his family, the days following their escape into the woods were a blur of survival. They moved cautiously, staying off the main roads and avoiding large towns, fearing what might await them there. They gathered what supplies they could from abandoned homes and stores, but each encounter with the remnants of normal life only deepened their sense of isolation.

News was scarce and unreliable. The few radio stations that still broadcasted were filled with conflicting reports and wild speculation. Some spoke of new leaders rising to restore order, while others warned of further chaos and impending doom. But one message was clear: the world was on the brink of a new era, one that would be defined by fear and uncertainty.

One morning, as John was carefully tuning the radio in the hope of finding some useful information, a voice crackled through the static. It was calm, authoritative, and chillingly confident—a stark contrast to the frantic broadcasts they had heard before.

"Citizens of the world," the voice began, "we are living in extraordinary times. The events of the past weeks have tested our faith and our resolve, but they have also provided us with an opportunity. An opportunity to build a new world, one that is free from the chaos of the past."

John leaned closer to the radio, his brow furrowing in concern. This was different. It wasn't just another panicked report or desperate plea for order. This was a declaration—a proclamation of power.

"As you know, millions have vanished," the voice continued, "but those of us who remain have been chosen. We have been given a second chance, a chance to create a world that is stronger, more unified, and more resilient. Under my leadership, we will rise from the ashes of this catastrophe and forge a new order—one that will ensure peace, prosperity, and security for all."

Emily entered the room, noticing the intense look on John's face. "What is it?" she asked quietly.

"Listen," John replied, motioning to the radio.

The voice continued, outlining a plan to restore order and rebuild society. It spoke of new laws, new systems of governance, and a global alliance that would bring all nations under a single, unified leadership. There was talk of rebuilding cities, reestablishing communication networks, and restoring essential services. It all sounded promising—on the surface.

But there was something in the tone, something in the way the voice spoke of power and control, that sent a chill down John's spine.

"We will no longer be divided by petty differences or regional conflicts," the voice declared. "We will stand as one people, under one banner, with one purpose. And together, we will ensure that nothing like this ever happens again."

The broadcast ended with a promise: a new era was beginning, and those who embraced it would thrive, while those who resisted would be left behind. The signal then faded into static, leaving John and Emily in stunned silence.

"Who was that?" Emily asked, her voice trembling slightly.

"I don't know," John replied, shaking his head. "But whoever it is, they've got power. And they're not afraid to use it."

Over the next few days, more broadcasts followed. The same voice—now identified as Alexander Mercer, a charismatic and influential figure who had risen to prominence in the wake of the disappearances—continued to outline his vision for the future. His message was one of unity and strength, but it was also laced with an undercurrent of control. It became clear that Mercer wasn't just trying to restore order; he was reshaping the world according to his own design.

John and Emily debated what to do next. Staying in the woods felt increasingly unsafe, especially as more people began to follow Mercer's call. They had heard rumors of gathering points, places where survivors were being taken to rebuild under the new order. But John was wary—everything about Mercer's message felt wrong to him, like a trap disguised as a lifeline.

"We need to find out more," John finally said. "We need to know what we're dealing with before we decide our next move."

Emily agreed, though the prospect of leaving their temporary shelter filled her with dread. The children were restless and scared, but they had to keep moving. Staying put wasn't an option.

As they packed up their meager belongings, John couldn't shake the feeling that they were being watched. The woods, once a refuge, now felt suffocating. Every rustle in the trees, every distant sound, made his heart race. The world was changing rapidly, and he feared they were running out of time to find a safe haven.

They traveled cautiously, sticking to backroads and avoiding populated areas as much as possible. But as they ventured closer to civilization, it became clear that the world they had once known was gone. The streets were patrolled by armed men, all wearing the same insignia—a stylized globe encircled by a laurel wreath. It was the symbol of Mercer's new order, a constant reminder of the power that was quickly consolidating.

In the towns they passed through, banners and posters proclaimed the dawn of a new era. "Unity," they declared. "Strength. Order." The words were everywhere, emblazoned on buildings and vehicles, broadcasted from loudspeakers. Mercer's face, stern and determined, stared down at them from billboards, his eyes seemingly following their every move.

It wasn't long before they encountered one of Mercer's patrols. The soldiers, efficient and emotionless, questioned them about their destination and purpose. John, doing his best to remain calm, explained that they were looking for a safe place to stay, somewhere to start over.

The patrol leader, a young man with cold, calculating eyes, studied them for a moment before nodding. "There's a settlement not far from here," he said. "They're taking in survivors. You can head there."

John thanked him, though the encounter left him unsettled. As they drove away, he glanced at Emily, who looked as uneasy as he felt.

"They're everywhere," she whispered. "How are we supposed to stay off their radar?"

"I don't know," John admitted. "But we have to keep moving. We can't afford to get caught up in this."

They continued on, following the patrol leader's directions but keeping a wary eye out for anything suspicious. The closer they got to the settlement, the more they saw signs of Mercer's influence. Makeshift checkpoints dotted the roads, manned by soldiers who were systematically organizing the flow of people into the area.

When they finally arrived at the settlement, they were struck by the stark contrast between the orderly, regimented camp and the chaos they had witnessed elsewhere. The settlement was well-organized, with rows of tents and temporary shelters set up in neat lines. People moved with purpose, following orders from officials who directed them to various stations—food distribution, medical care, registration.

John and Emily hesitated at the entrance, unsure of whether to enter. The settlement offered security, but it also meant submitting to Mercer's control. It was a difficult choice—risk the unknown, or take shelter in a place where their every move would be monitored.

As they stood there, deliberating, a group of soldiers approached. One of them, a woman with a stern expression, stepped forward. "Welcome," she said, her tone more commanding than welcoming. "You'll need to register and receive your assignment. Follow me."

John exchanged a glance with Emily, who nodded slightly. They had no choice—they would have to play along, at least for now.

The soldier led them through the camp, explaining the rules as they walked. Everyone was required to contribute to the settlement's upkeep, whether through labor, skills, or other means. There were curfews, checkpoints, and regular inspections. Disobedience was not tolerated.

They were registered by a tired-looking clerk who took down their names and assigned them to a small tent on the outskirts of the camp. As they were led to their new home, John couldn't shake the feeling that they were walking into a trap. The settlement was orderly, but it was also suffocating—a place where free will was being slowly eroded in the name of survival.

As they settled into their tent, John sat down heavily, the weight of their situation pressing down on him. They were safe, for now, but at what cost? The world was changing around them, and Mercer's vision for the future was becoming a reality. It was a world of control, of order imposed through fear and power.

Emily sat beside him, placing a hand on his shoulder. "We'll figure this out," she said softly, though her voice betrayed her own doubts.

John nodded, though he wasn't sure how. The old world was gone, replaced by a new order that was tightening its grip with every passing day. They had to stay vigilant, to find a way to survive without losing themselves in the process.

But as John looked around the camp, at the faces of those who had already resigned themselves to Mercer's rule, he realized how difficult that would be. The new order was here, and it was growing stronger. The question now was whether they could find a way to resist—or if they, too, would be consumed by the darkness that was spreading across the world.

The sense of resignation was palpable, a quiet acceptance of their new reality. People moved about their assigned tasks with mechanical efficiency, their eyes downcast, their expressions hollow. It was as if the spark of individuality, of hope, had been extinguished.

John knew that they couldn't afford to fall into the same trap. They had to keep their minds sharp, their spirits strong. But in a world where every decision, every action, was dictated by a central authority, maintaining a sense of autonomy would be a constant struggle.

The first night in the camp was restless. The sounds of the settlement—footsteps of patrolling soldiers, the distant hum of generators, and the occasional murmur of voices—kept them on edge. John lay awake, staring at the tent's ceiling, his thoughts racing. He couldn't help but wonder what the future held for them, for their children, and for the world at large.

Morning came too quickly, bringing with it the harsh realities of life under the new order. They were awakened by a loud horn that blared throughout the camp, signaling the start of the day. They were expected to report to their assigned stations immediately after breakfast, and the schedule was strict. There was little time for anything other than work and the bare necessities of life.

John was assigned to a construction crew, tasked with expanding the settlement's perimeter and fortifying its defenses. The work was grueling, made more difficult by the constant surveillance of the overseers, who monitored every move with cold precision. The crew worked in near silence, too afraid to speak freely, their thoughts carefully guarded.

Emily, meanwhile, was placed in the medical tent, helping to care for the sick and injured. The conditions were rudimentary, with limited supplies and overworked staff, but Emily did her best to bring some comfort to those in need. It was hard, though, to offer hope in a place where despair was so pervasive.

The days blurred together, each one much like the last, marked by an oppressive routine that left little room for anything beyond survival. John and Emily spoke in hushed tones at night, their conversations always returning to the same question: how could they escape this life? How could they break free from the iron grip of the new order?

As the days turned into weeks, they began to notice small signs of resistance within the camp. A whispered conversation here, a furtive glance there—there were others who, like them, were not content to simply obey. It was a glimmer of hope in an otherwise bleak existence, and John latched onto it.

One evening, as they were returning to their tent after the day's work, John noticed a man lingering near the edge of the camp. The man, who had been watching them for several days, finally approached. His appearance was unremarkable, but his eyes were sharp, and there was a quiet intensity about him.

"Carter, right?" the man asked in a low voice, glancing around to ensure they weren't being watched.

John nodded cautiously. "Who's asking?"

"My name's Michael," the man replied, his tone measured. "I've been watching you and your family. You don't belong here, do you?"

John stiffened, his guard immediately up. "What do you mean?"

Michael leaned in closer, his voice barely above a whisper. "I mean, you're not like the others. You're not content to just fall in line and do as you're told. You're looking for a way out."

John didn't respond immediately, weighing his options. Trust was a rare commodity in the camp, and he couldn't afford to be careless. But something about Michael's demeanor suggested that he might be an ally, someone who could help them.

"What do you want?" John asked, his voice steady but guarded.

"To help you," Michael replied simply. "There are others here, like us, who don't want to live under Mercer's rule. We're planning something—a way to break free from this place. But we need people we can trust."

John exchanged a glance with Emily, who nodded subtly. They had to take a chance, to trust that Michael was telling the truth. The alternative—remaining trapped in the camp, slowly losing their will to resist—was unthinkable.

"What do you need us to do?" John asked, his resolve hardening.

"Meet me tomorrow night, after curfew," Michael instructed. "There's a storage shed near the east fence. Be there, and come alone."

With that, Michael slipped away into the shadows, leaving John and Emily with more questions than answers. They returned to their tent, their minds racing. Could they really trust Michael? Was this their chance to escape, or was it a trap set by Mercer's enforcers to root out dissent?

Despite the risks, they knew they had to act. The thought of remaining in the camp, of slowly losing their freedom and their identities, was too much to bear. They couldn't allow their children to grow up in a world where fear and control were the only constants.

The next day passed in a haze of anxiety and anticipation. John and Emily went through the motions, careful not to arouse suspicion, but their thoughts were entirely focused on the meeting that night. Every glance from a soldier, every whispered conversation, felt like a potential threat.

When night finally fell, John waited until the camp had quieted down, the only sounds the distant patrols and the rustling of the wind. He slipped out of the tent, careful not to wake the children, and made his way toward the storage shed. The darkness was oppressive, the moon hidden behind thick clouds, but John moved with purpose, his heart pounding in his chest.

As he approached the shed, he saw Michael waiting in the shadows, along with two other figures. John hesitated for a moment, then steeled himself and stepped forward.

"You came," Michael said, a note of approval in his voice. "Good."

The two others stepped forward as well—a woman in her thirties with a determined look, and an older man with a hardened expression. Michael introduced them as Sarah and David, both of whom had been in the camp for several months.

"We've been planning this for a while," Sarah explained, her voice low but intense. "Mercer's grip is tightening, and we need to act before it's too late. We've identified a weak point in the camp's defenses—a place where the fence is old and poorly maintained. If we can breach it, we can escape into the woods and make our way to a safe house we've set up."

"It won't be easy," David added, his tone grim. "The patrols are heavy, and the risk of getting caught is high. But it's our only chance."

John listened carefully, weighing their words. It was a dangerous plan, but it was also their best hope of escaping the nightmare they were living in. He glanced back at the camp, at the rows of tents and the ever-watchful eyes of Mercer's soldiers. There was no future for them here—only a slow, suffocating death of the spirit.

"I'm in," John said finally, his voice firm.

Michael nodded, a small smile playing on his lips. "Good. We'll make our move tomorrow night. Be ready."

With that, the group dispersed, slipping back into the shadows. John returned to the tent, his mind racing with thoughts of the upcoming escape. It was a gamble, but it was one they had to take. The alternative was unthinkable.

The next day was agonizingly slow, each minute dragging by as John and Emily prepared for what could be their last day in the camp. They kept their heads down, going through the motions of their assigned tasks, but their minds were focused on the night ahead.

As darkness fell, the camp settled into its usual routine. The patrols were out in force, their flashlights cutting through the night as they made their rounds. John and Emily waited, tense and alert, until the moment came to make their move.

With a final glance at their sleeping children, they slipped out of the tent and made their way to the rendezvous point. Michael, Sarah, and David were already there, their expressions grim and determined. The group exchanged nods, and then, without a word, they set off toward the weak point in the fence.

The night was eerily quiet, the only sounds the rustling of leaves and the distant hum of generators. The group moved swiftly but cautiously, staying low and avoiding the patrols as they approached the fence. John's heart was pounding, every nerve on edge as they reached the weak spot—a section where the metal had rusted and the wires were loose.

David pulled out a pair of wire cutters, and with quick, practiced movements, he began snipping through the fence. The others kept watch, their eyes scanning the darkness for any sign of movement. John could feel the tension in the air, the weight of what they were about to do pressing down on him.

Finally, the last wire was cut, and the group slipped through the gap in the fence, one by one. They moved quickly, leaving the camp behind as they disappeared into the woods. The trees closed in around them, offering a sense of cover, but also a new set of dangers.

They moved through the forest in silence, each of them hyper-aware of their surroundings. The journey to the safe house would take several hours, and the risk of being discovered was high. But for the first time in weeks, John felt a glimmer of hope. They were out of the camp, free from Mercer's control—at least for now.

As they pressed on, John couldn't help but think of the others they had left behind. The camp, with its rigid order and crushing conformity, was a symbol of the new world Mercer was building. A world where freedom was sacrificed for security, where obedience was the highest virtue.

Every snap of a twig, every rustle of leaves sent their hearts racing, but they pressed on, driven by the desperation to escape the life they had left behind.

As they moved deeper into the forest, the moon emerged from behind the clouds, casting a faint silver light on their path. The group moved in single file, careful not to leave a trace of their passage. Michael led the way, his familiarity with the terrain evident in the surety of his steps. John and Emily followed closely behind, with Sarah and David bringing up the rear.

After what felt like an eternity, Michael signaled for them to stop. They huddled together in a small clearing, the trees forming a natural barrier against prying eyes. Michael pointed to a narrow trail that wound its way through the underbrush.

"This trail leads to the safe house," he whispered, his voice barely audible above the sound of the wind. "We're close, but we need to be careful. There could be patrols in the area."

The group nodded in agreement, their resolve unwavering. They had come too far to turn back now.

The trail was narrow and uneven, making progress slow and treacherous. The dense foliage around them muffled their footsteps, but it also made it difficult to see more than a few feet ahead. John's senses were on high alert, every shadow and sound seeming to hide potential danger.

As they continued, the trail began to widen, and the trees thinned out slightly, allowing more moonlight to filter through. The air was cooler here, and the scent of pine needles filled their lungs, a welcome change from the stifling atmosphere of the camp.

Suddenly, Michael froze, holding up a hand to signal the others to stop. They all came to a halt, their breaths caught in their throats. In the distance, barely visible through the trees, they could make out the faint glow of a flashlight.

John's heart pounded in his chest. Had they been spotted? Was this the end of their escape?

Michael motioned for them to move off the trail and into the cover of the underbrush. They crouched low, barely daring to breathe as the light drew closer. John could hear the crunch of boots on the forest floor, the sound growing louder with each passing moment.

The group huddled together, their bodies tense with anticipation. The light wavered, sweeping across the trail and the surrounding trees, as if searching for something—or someone. John's mind raced with fear. If they were discovered now, there would be no escape.

The light hovered for a moment, and then, to their immense relief, it began to move away, the footsteps receding into the distance. The group remained still, not

The group remained still until the footsteps faded completely. Once it was safe, Michael signaled for them to continue. They moved cautiously, the near miss heightening their awareness.

After another hour of careful trekking, they finally reached the safe house—a small, dilapidated cabin hidden deep within the forest. It was far from luxurious, but it offered shelter and, most importantly, safety.

Inside, the group collapsed onto the worn furniture, exhaustion finally catching up with them. Michael went over the plan for the days ahead, stressing the importance of staying hidden and gathering supplies. The journey was far from over, but for the first time in weeks, they felt a glimmer of hope.

As they settled in for the night, John and Emily exchanged a look. They had escaped the camp, but the fight for freedom was just beginning. Whatever lay ahead, they knew they would face it together.

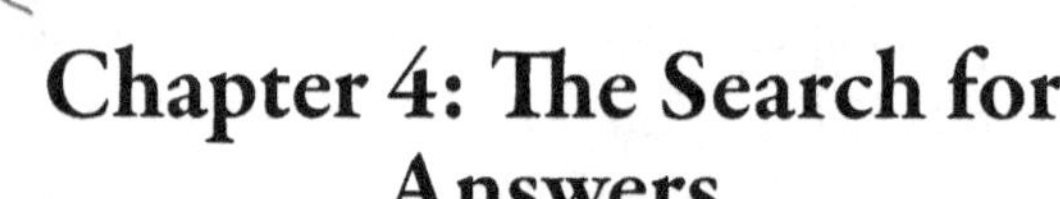

Chapter 4: The Search for Answers

THE MORNING SUNLIGHT filtered through the cracks in the cabin's weathered walls, casting slivers of light across the room. John sat at the small, rickety table, his Bible open in front of him. He hadn't slept much. His mind was a whirlpool of questions, doubts, and fears, all of them circling around the same, unshakable thought: Why had this happened, and what was coming next?

Emily approached quietly, placing a hand on his shoulder. "You've been reading that since dawn," she said softly.

John nodded, not lifting his eyes from the pages. "I'm trying to understand, Em. I need to know what we're up against."

"Have you found anything?" she asked, though she already knew the answer from his troubled expression.

John sighed deeply. "The prophecies... they're all there. The signs, the warnings. But I never imagined it would be like this—so sudden, so terrifying."

Emily pulled up a chair and sat next to him. "I'm scared too, John. But we're alive, and we've got the kids. That's what matters right now."

John reached out, taking her hand in his. "I know. But we need to prepare. We need to understand what's happening so we can protect them, so we can survive."

Before they could continue, there was a soft knock on the door. Michael entered, followed by Sarah and David. The children were still rubbing sleep from their eyes, their faces pale from the events of the past days.

"We need to talk," Michael said, his tone serious. He gestured for them to gather around the table. Once they were all seated, he leaned forward, his voice low and urgent.

"We're safe for now, but that won't last. The world is changing fast, and we need to be ready for what's coming. We can't just hide out here forever."

"What do you suggest?" John asked, already dreading the answer.

"We need information," Michael replied. "We need to find out what's really going on out there—who's in control, what the government is doing, how people are reacting. If we're going to survive, we can't be in the dark."

John nodded in agreement. "But where do we start? The last thing we heard on the radio was chaos—no one seemed to know what was happening."

Michael pulled out a map and spread it across the table. "There's a small town not far from here. It's isolated, but there's a church there, and I know the pastor. He's a good man, and if anyone can give us answers, it's him."

"A church?" Emily asked, frowning. "Do you think they'll have any more answers than we do?"

"Maybe," Michael said. "But it's not just about answers. It's about finding people we can trust, building connections. We can't do this alone."

John looked at the map, tracing the route with his finger. The town was about a day's walk away, through the dense forest and over rough terrain. It was a risk, but staying in the cabin indefinitely was not an option.

"We'll go," John decided, looking up at Michael. "But we need to be careful. If they're looking for us..."

"We'll be careful," Michael assured him. "We'll move at night, keep off the main roads. But we need to make contact with others. We can't do this on our own."

Sarah, who had been silent until now, spoke up. "What if it's dangerous? What if... what if there are more of those people out there, the ones with the flashlights?"

John turned to his daughter, seeing the fear in her eyes. "We'll be careful, Sarah. We won't take any unnecessary risks. But we need to do this—for all of us."

David, who had been listening quietly, nodded. "I'll help. I'm not a kid anymore. I can do something."

Emily smiled faintly at her son's determination, but worry creased her brow. "We'll all help," she said. "But we stick together, no matter what."

Michael folded up the map and stood. "We leave tonight. Get some rest, gather what you can carry. We need to be ready to move as soon as it's dark."

The family dispersed to prepare, the weight of the decision settling over them like a heavy blanket. As John packed their few belongings, his thoughts drifted back to the Bible on the table. The prophecies had foretold a time of great tribulation, of darkness and despair. But they also spoke of hope, of a final victory for those who remained steadfast.

He clung to that hope now, even as the world crumbled around them.

Night fell, and the forest came alive with the sounds of nocturnal creatures. The group moved silently through the underbrush, keeping to the shadows. Michael led the way, his military training evident in the way he navigated the terrain.

It was a long, arduous journey, the darkness pressing in on them from all sides. The children struggled to keep up, but they never complained, their fear driving them forward.

As they neared the town, the sounds of civilization—distant cars, muffled voices—began to reach their ears. Michael signaled for them to stop, and they huddled together just outside the tree line, peering down at the small cluster of buildings.

The town was eerily quiet, its streets deserted. A few lights flickered in windows, but there was no sign of life. The church, a small, white building with a steeple, stood at the center, its doors closed.

"We'll head straight to the church," Michael whispered. "Stay close, and be ready for anything."

They moved cautiously down the hill, sticking to the shadows. The air was thick with tension as they crossed the empty streets, their footsteps echoing in the silence.

When they reached the church, Michael knocked softly on the door. For a moment, there was no response. Then, the door creaked open, revealing an older man with graying hair and tired eyes.

"Michael," the man said, relief washing over his features. "I was beginning to think no one would come."

"We're here now, Pastor," Michael replied. "And we need your help."

The pastor stepped aside, allowing them to enter. Inside, the church was dimly lit by a few candles, the pews empty. The smell of incense hung in the air, a faint reminder of the services that had once been held here.

The pastor led them to a small room at the back of the church, where a few other people were gathered. They looked up as the group entered, their faces a mixture of fear and hope.

"We've been waiting," the pastor said, closing the door behind them. "The world is changing, and we need to be ready. But first, you need to know the truth."

John exchanged a glance with Emily, his heart pounding. This was what they had been searching for—answers, guidance, a way forward. But as the pastor began to speak, revealing the extent of the darkness that had engulfed the world, John realized that the truth was more terrifying than he had ever imagined.

The Rapture had come, and with it, the dawn of a new and terrible era. The Antichrist was rising, and the battle for the souls of humanity had just begun.

The pastor's voice was grave as he began to recount the events that had unfolded since the Rapture. His words were heavy with the weight of what was to come, each sentence like a blow to the fragile hope that John had clung to.

"The world is in chaos," the pastor said, his eyes scanning the room. "The disappearances have left nations in disarray. Governments are struggling to maintain control, and people are desperate for answers, for leadership."

John listened intently, absorbing every word. He could see the truth of the pastor's statements reflected in the haunted eyes of the people around him—men and women who had lost loved ones, who had witnessed the unraveling of society firsthand.

"The Antichrist," the pastor continued, "is rising to power. He hasn't revealed himself fully yet, but his influence is spreading. People are being deceived, drawn in by promises of peace and security. But it's all a lie—a trap to ensnare the world in darkness."

Emily tightened her grip on John's hand. The thought of such evil, so calculated and pervasive, sent a chill down her spine. "How do we stop him?" she asked, her voice barely above a whisper.

The pastor shook his head. "Stopping him isn't possible. The Scriptures tell us that his reign is inevitable, part of the divine plan. But there is hope. Those who remain faithful, who refuse to bow to his rule, will be saved in the end. Our task is to resist, to stand firm in our faith, no matter the cost."

One of the other men in the room, a tall, broad-shouldered man with a military bearing, spoke up. "But how do we resist? The world is falling apart. We don't have the resources, the numbers..."

"We have something more powerful than any weapon or army," the pastor interjected, his voice filled with conviction. "We have the truth, and we have our faith. That is our greatest strength."

The man looked unconvinced, but he remained silent, his expression grim. John understood his skepticism. How could faith alone stand against the tide of darkness that was sweeping the world? But then he remembered the prophecy, the promise that those who endured would be saved. It was a small comfort, but it was all they had.

The pastor continued, outlining their plan. They would form a network of believers, spreading information, gathering resources, and offering refuge to those who sought to escape the Antichrist's influence. It was a dangerous mission, one that would require immense courage and sacrifice.

"We'll need to be careful," the pastor warned. "There are those who have already fallen under the Antichrist's spell, who would betray us in a heartbeat. We must be vigilant, trusting only those we know are true."

John nodded, feeling the weight of responsibility settling on his shoulders. This was more than just survival now. This was a battle for the soul of humanity, and he was determined to fight with everything he had.

"Where do we start?" Michael asked, his tone steady and resolute.

"There are pockets of resistance forming in other towns," the pastor replied. "We need to make contact with them, establish a communication network. It won't be easy—travel is dangerous, and the authorities are cracking down on any group activity. But it's the only way we'll stand a chance."

Michael turned to John, a question in his eyes. "Are you with us?"

John hesitated for only a moment before nodding. "Yes. We'll do whatever it takes."

Emily looked at him, her eyes filled with both fear and determination. "We'll stand together, John. Whatever happens."

The pastor smiled faintly, a glimmer of hope in his weary eyes. "Then we have a chance. With God's guidance, we can face whatever comes. But we must be prepared for the trials ahead. The Antichrist's power is growing, and the world will soon be plunged into darkness like we've never seen before."

The rest of the night was spent in planning. The group discussed logistics, mapped out routes, and assigned tasks. John was put in charge of finding a way to communicate with the other resistance groups, while Michael would lead the effort to gather supplies.

As the hours passed, the initial shock of the situation began to give way to a steely resolve. They were a small group, but they were determined. They would not let fear paralyze them, nor would they succumb to the despair that had claimed so many others.

Finally, as dawn began to break, the meeting came to an end. The pastor led them in a quiet prayer, asking for strength and guidance in the days ahead. When the prayer was over, the group began to disperse, each person heading to their assigned task.

John lingered in the church for a moment, his thoughts racing. The world outside was still and quiet, but he knew that peace was an illusion. The real battle was just beginning, and it would take everything they had to survive it.

As he walked back to the cabin with Emily and the children, John felt a renewed sense of purpose. The road ahead would be fraught with danger, but they were not alone. They had each other, and they had their faith. And that, he hoped, would be enough to see them through.

Later that day, as John sat outside the cabin, watching the sun rise over the horizon, he couldn't help but think of the prophecy once more. The words of Scripture echoed in his mind, a reminder of the trials that lay ahead:

"For then shall be great tribulation, such as was not since the beginning of the world to this time, no, nor ever shall be." (Matthew 24:21)

The world was on the brink of an unprecedented era of darkness. But John knew that, just as the prophecy foretold great tribulation, it also spoke of deliverance. He held onto that promise, clinging to it like a lifeline.

Whatever came next, they would face it together, guided by the light of their faith in a world that seemed to be drowning in shadows.

The journey back to the cabin was filled with an uneasy silence. The children, Sarah and David, had sensed the tension, their usual chatter subdued. Emily walked beside John, her hand in his, both of them lost in their own thoughts. The pastor's words hung in the air between them, a heavy reminder of the responsibility they now bore.

As they approached the cabin, the familiar sight of their home brought a fleeting sense of comfort, but it quickly faded as the reality of their situation settled in. The world they had known was gone, replaced by uncertainty and fear. Yet, they had a purpose now—a mission to resist the darkness spreading across the globe.

Inside the cabin, the family gathered around the kitchen table. John had insisted on discussing their next steps openly, even with the children present. They needed to understand the gravity of what was happening and the dangers they would face.

"Sarah, David," John began, his voice gentle but firm, "we need to talk about what's going on. Things are going to be different from now on, and we all have to be prepared."

Sarah, the older of the two, looked at her father with wide, worried eyes. "Is it because of what the pastor said? About the bad man taking over?"

John exchanged a glance with Emily before nodding. "Yes, sweetheart. There's a man—someone very powerful—who's trying to take control of everything. But we're not going to let that happen. We're going to fight back, in our own way."

David, younger and more innocent, frowned in confusion. "But why, Daddy? Why would anyone want to do something so mean?"

John's heart ached at the question, wishing he could shield his son from the harsh truths of the world. "Some people," he said carefully, "are blinded by their own desires. They want power, and they don't care who they hurt to get it. But we're not alone. There are others like us, people who believe in doing what's right, and we're going to find them."

Emily reached out, placing a comforting hand on David's shoulder. "We're going to be careful, and we're going to stick together. No matter what happens, we'll get through this as a family."

Sarah, always the more perceptive of the two, asked, "What do we have to do?"

John took a deep breath, grateful for his daughter's strength. "We're going to be part of a group—people who are resisting this man's influence. We'll need to be careful about who we trust and where we go. It's going to be dangerous, but it's important."

The children were silent for a moment, processing this new reality. Then, with the resolve that only children can muster in the face of fear, Sarah nodded. "Okay. We'll help."

David, though still clearly frightened, nodded as well. "Yeah, we'll help, Daddy."

John felt a swell of pride in his children. They were so young, yet they understood the seriousness of what was happening. He reached out, pulling both of them into a tight embrace. "Thank you. We're going to need each other more than ever."

The rest of the day was spent in preparation. John and Emily took inventory of their supplies, carefully considering what they would need in the coming weeks. They sorted through food, water, and other essentials, knowing they might have to leave at a moment's notice.

John also began working on a plan to establish communication with the other resistance groups. The pastor had mentioned a network forming in nearby towns, and John knew that coordinating with them would be crucial. But with communication systems being monitored and travel becoming increasingly dangerous, it wouldn't be easy.

That evening, as the sun dipped below the horizon, casting long shadows across the forest, John sat outside the cabin, working on a makeshift radio. He had some experience with electronics from his days working on construction sites, and he hoped that he could rig something together that would allow them to stay in contact with other survivors.

Emily joined him after putting the children to bed. She sat beside him, watching as he fiddled with wires and circuits, his brow furrowed in concentration.

"Do you really think this will work?" she asked quietly.

John didn't look up from his work. "I hope so. If we can make contact, it'll give us a fighting chance. We can't do this alone, Emily. We need to know what's happening out there, where it's safe to go, and who we can trust."

Emily nodded, though she couldn't hide the fear in her eyes. "I just worry... what if we're discovered? What if they find out we're trying to resist?"

John paused, setting down the wires, and looked at his wife. "That's a risk we have to take. We can't just sit back and do nothing. If we don't fight back, if we don't try to protect what's left of our world, then we've already lost."

She sighed, leaning into him. "I know. I just... I'm scared, John. For the kids, for us... everything is changing so fast."

He wrapped an arm around her, pulling her close. "I'm scared too. But we're strong, Emily. We've always been strong. We'll get through this. We have to believe that."

They sat in silence for a while, the only sound the faint hum of the radio as John continued his work. The night air was cool, a sharp contrast to the tension that hung in the air. But despite the fear, there was also a flicker of hope—a small, stubborn flame that refused to be extinguished.

As the hours passed and the night deepened, John finally managed to get a faint signal on the radio. It was scratchy and distorted, but it was there—a lifeline in the darkness.

He and Emily exchanged a look, the weight of what they had just accomplished settling in. They had taken the first step in what would undoubtedly be a long and dangerous journey. But for now, it was enough.

John adjusted the radio, trying to clear the signal, and then he spoke into the microphone. "This is John Carter, broadcasting from Mill Creek. If anyone can hear me, we're here. We're ready to fight. Over."

For a long moment, there was only static. But then, faintly, a voice crackled through the speaker.

"This is the Westbrook group. We hear you, Mill Creek. Stand by for further instructions."

John felt a surge of relief. They weren't alone. There were others out there, others who had refused to bow to the rising darkness.

Emily squeezed his hand, and John nodded, his resolve hardening. The battle was far from over, but they had just made their first connection, their first step toward resistance.

As they turned off the radio and prepared to head inside, John looked out into the night, a sense of determination filling him. They would fight, they would resist, and no matter what came next, they would do everything in their power to protect their family and their faith.

The world was changing, but they were ready. Together, they would face whatever trials lay ahead, guided by the light of their belief in a world that had seemingly forgotten what it meant to hope.

Chapter 5: The Revelation

THE DAYS THAT FOLLOWED their initial contact with the Westbrook group were a blur of preparation and planning. John Carter found himself consumed by the tasks at hand, but beneath the surface, a nagging sense of unease festered. The world outside their cabin had grown eerily quiet, as if holding its breath in anticipation of what was to come.

Emily, ever perceptive, noticed the change in her husband. "John," she said one evening as they sat together in the dim light of the kitchen, the children already asleep. "You've been distant. What's going on?"

John hesitated, running a hand through his hair. "I don't know, Emily. It's just... something doesn't feel right. I keep thinking about the pastor's words, about the prophecies we've been hearing about. It feels like we're missing something—like there's a piece of the puzzle we haven't found yet."

Emily reached across the table, taking his hand in hers. "Maybe it's time we looked for it, then."

Her words struck a chord with John. He had been so focused on the practical aspects of survival—food, water, communication—that he hadn't considered the spiritual implications as deeply as he should have. The pastor had hinted at ancient texts, prophecies that might shed light on what was happening. Perhaps it was time to explore that avenue further.

The next morning, after ensuring the children were occupied, John and Emily made the decision to revisit Pastor Williams. The old church, nestled on the outskirts of the town, was one of the few places left untouched by the chaos that had engulfed the world. It stood as a beacon of hope and a sanctuary for those seeking answers.

As they arrived at the church, the familiar sight of the weathered building brought a sense of calm to John's troubled mind. The wooden doors creaked as they pushed them open, stepping into the cool, shadowed interior. The pews were empty, save for a few scattered Bibles, their pages worn from years of use.

Pastor Williams was at the altar, deep in prayer. He looked up as they approached, a serene expression on his face. "John, Emily," he greeted them warmly. "What brings you here today?"

John didn't waste time with pleasantries. "Pastor, we need to know more about the prophecies you mentioned. We've been hearing things—about the Rapture, about the Antichrist. I feel like we're standing on the edge of something monumental, and we're blind to what's really happening."

The pastor nodded, as if he had expected this. "Come with me," he said, leading them toward a small room at the back of the church.

The room was filled with shelves of books, old and new, their spines cracked and faded. In the center of the room was a large wooden table, covered in scrolls, papers, and ancient texts. Pastor Williams gestured for them to sit.

"This," he began, spreading out one of the scrolls, "is where we begin to understand the larger picture. The events we are witnessing have been foretold in these texts—some as old as time itself. The Rapture, the rise of the Antichrist, the tribulations... they're all here."

John and Emily leaned in, their eyes scanning the pages as the pastor continued. "These prophecies are not just warnings; they're a roadmap. A guide to what is happening and what is yet to come. But interpreting them is not easy. They are shrouded in symbolism and metaphor, meant to be understood only by those who seek the truth with an open heart."

Emily's voice was quiet, reverent. "What do they say about what's happening now?"

Pastor Williams sighed, his fingers tracing the ancient script. "The prophecies speak of a time when the world will be tested, when a great darkness will fall over the earth, and only those with unwavering faith will endure. The Rapture is just the beginning—the first step in a series of events that will challenge the very fabric of humanity."

John frowned, his mind racing. "And the Antichrist? Where does he fit into all this?"

The pastor's expression grew grave. "The Antichrist is prophesied to rise during this time of chaos, presenting himself as a savior, a beacon of hope in a world gone mad. But he is the great deceiver, leading many astray with promises of peace and prosperity. His true nature will only be revealed to those who are vigilant, those who can see beyond his lies."

Emily shuddered, her grip tightening on John's hand. "How do we know who he is?"

Pastor Williams looked at them with piercing eyes. "He will be charismatic, a leader who rises from the ashes of the old world. He will bring unity to the nations, but his power will come at a great cost. The signs will be subtle at first—a shift in the political landscape, a sudden peace agreement that seems too good to be true. But as his influence grows, so too will the darkness he brings."

John sat back, the weight of the pastor's words pressing down on him. This was more than he had anticipated—more than just a fight for survival. This was a battle for the soul of the world, a fight against an enemy that could not be defeated by force alone.

Pastor Williams continued, his voice steady and calm. "The key to recognizing the Antichrist lies in the scriptures. There are passages that speak of his rise, his methods, and ultimately, his downfall. But these passages are scattered throughout the Bible, hidden within other prophecies. We must study them, learn from them, and prepare ourselves for what is to come."

Emily looked at John, her eyes filled with determination. "We have to do this, John. We can't just sit back and wait for things to unfold. We have to be ready."

John nodded, the resolve in his heart solidifying. "You're right. We need to understand these prophecies, to see the patterns, to know what's coming. It's the only way we can protect our family—and maybe even save others."

The rest of the day was spent in the church, pouring over ancient texts and scriptures. Pastor Williams guided them through the labyrinth of prophecies, explaining the significance of each passage, the historical context, and how they might relate to current events.

As the sun dipped low in the sky, casting long shadows through the stained-glass windows, John and Emily began to piece together a picture—fragmented and incomplete, but enough to see the outlines of what was coming. They learned of the seven seals, the trumpets of judgment, and the bowls of wrath that would be poured out upon the earth. They read of the false peace that would precede a time of unparalleled suffering, and of the faithful remnant who would endure to the end.

It was overwhelming, terrifying even, but it also gave them a sense of purpose. They were not just passive observers in this unfolding drama—they had a role to play, a responsibility to act.

As they prepared to leave the church, Pastor Williams placed a hand on John's shoulder. "Remember, John, knowledge is your greatest weapon. But it is also a burden. Use it wisely, and never lose sight of the truth."

John met the pastor's gaze, a silent understanding passing between them. "Thank you, Pastor. We won't forget."

The drive back to the cabin was filled with quiet reflection. The weight of what they had learned pressed heavily on their minds, but there was also a flicker of hope. They had a direction now, a path to follow. And as long as they held onto their faith, they believed they could weather the storm that was coming.

That night, after tucking the children into bed, John and Emily sat together in the living room, the fire crackling softly in the hearth. They spoke in hushed tones, sharing their thoughts, their fears, and their hopes for the future.

"We need to start gathering people," John said finally. "Others who believe, who want to resist. We can't do this alone."

Emily nodded in agreement. "The Westbrook group is a start, but we'll need more. We'll have to be careful, though. The pastor said the Antichrist will have many followers, people who will do anything to stop us."

"We'll find a way," John said with determination. "We have to. For our children, for our faith... for the world."

They fell silent, listening to the wind howling outside, a reminder of the growing chaos beyond their walls. But inside, they were united, their resolve stronger than ever.

As the fire burned low and the night grew deeper, John reached for Emily's hand, holding it tightly. "Whatever happens," he said softly, "we'll face it together."

Emily squeezed his hand, a small smile playing on her lips. "Together."

And with that, they prepared to face whatever trials lay ahead, their faith unshaken, their hearts resolute. The storm was coming, but they would stand firm, guided by the revelations they had uncovered, and the unyielding belief that they were on the right side of history.

As the days wore on, John and Emily found themselves deeply engrossed in their study of the ancient prophecies. Their days were filled with reading, analyzing, and discussing the revelations they had uncovered. Despite the growing chaos outside, the cabin became a sanctuary of hope and determination.

One evening, as John was poring over a particularly cryptic passage, Emily's voice interrupted his thoughts. "John, come look at this."

He looked up, curious, and saw Emily holding an old, tattered book. Its cover was worn, and the pages had yellowed with age. "What is it?" he asked, taking the book from her.

Emily opened it carefully, revealing an old handwritten manuscript. "I found this in one of the church's side rooms. It looks like it might be a commentary on the Book of Revelation. It's not in the same shape as the other texts we saw."

John scanned the manuscript's contents. The handwriting was meticulous, and the pages were filled with notes and underlined passages. The commentary seemed to offer interpretations of the more obscure passages of Revelation, linking them to historical events and current circumstances.

As John read through the manuscript, a particular passage caught his eye:

"And I saw, and behold a white horse: and he that sat on him had a bow; and a crown was given unto him: and he went forth conquering, and to conquer."

John frowned, deep in thought. "This is referring to the first seal. The rider on the white horse is often interpreted as the Antichrist, or at least a precursor to his rise."

Emily nodded. "That fits with what we've seen. The rise of the charismatic leader who promises peace and unity. But the manuscript adds something interesting."

She pointed to another note:

"The white horse symbolizes false peace. Beware the one who comes promising salvation while sowing the seeds of destruction. His true nature will be revealed through the ensuing chaos."

John leaned back, his mind racing. "So, the rider isn't just about a leader—he's about deception. And the chaos that follows is part of revealing his true nature."

Emily's expression was pensive. "If we're right, then the Antichrist's true intentions will become clear as the world descends further into chaos. But how do we prepare for that?"

John's gaze settled on a passage that spoke of the need for vigilance and wisdom. "We need to stay informed, connected with others who understand these prophecies. And we need to be prepared for the aftermath of the Antichrist's rise. The next seals, the disasters—they're all part of the plan."

The following days were spent gathering and organizing the information they had found. They reached out to their contacts, including the Westbrook group, to share their findings and discuss strategies for the impending crisis.

One evening, as John and Emily were going over their notes, a knock on the door interrupted them. John cautiously approached and opened it to find Pastor Williams standing outside, his expression serious.

"Pastor Williams," John greeted, stepping aside to let him in. "What brings you here?"

The pastor entered, looking weary but resolute. "I've come to share something important. I've been doing some research of my own, and I've discovered something that might change everything."

John and Emily exchanged a glance and then ushered the pastor to a seat. "What have you found?"

Pastor Williams sat down, his eyes grave. "There are additional prophecies, lesser-known but significant. They speak of a time when the Antichrist will perform signs and wonders, deceiving even the elect if possible. These miracles will be used to solidify his power and control."

John frowned, absorbing the implications. "So, the Antichrist will use deception on a grand scale. We need to be vigilant about the signs and miracles he might perform."

"Yes," Pastor Williams confirmed. "And there's more. According to these prophecies, the Antichrist will establish a false peace and demand worship from all nations. The Book of Revelation speaks of a mark that will be required for buying and selling—a mark that signifies allegiance to the Antichrist."

Emily's face paled slightly. "A mark? How will we recognize it?"

Pastor Williams nodded. "The mark will be visible, likely on the hand or forehead. It will be a symbol of loyalty to the Antichrist's regime. Those who refuse to take it will face persecution and hardship."

John's mind raced with the implications. "We need to prepare for this. If the Antichrist's control becomes so pervasive, we'll have to find ways to live outside his system, to resist his demands."

Pastor Williams agreed. "We must also remember that the prophecies speak of a remnant, those who will remain faithful despite the trials. We need to build a network, support one another, and stay true to our faith."

John and Emily exchanged determined glances. "We'll do everything we can," John said firmly. "We'll find others who believe, who are willing to resist and fight for what's right."

The pastor offered a small, reassuring smile. "I have faith in you. The path ahead will be difficult, but you are not alone. Remember, the light shines brightest in the darkest times."

With those words, Pastor Williams left, leaving John and Emily with a renewed sense of purpose. They had a clearer understanding of the challenges they would face and the importance of their mission.

That night, as they sat together, reflecting on the revelations, John felt a deep sense of resolve. They had uncovered vital information, but the road ahead was still fraught with danger and uncertainty. Yet, in the face of overwhelming odds, they were ready to confront whatever lay ahead.

Emily looked at John, her eyes full of unwavering support. "We'll get through this, John. We have each other, and we have our faith. That's more powerful than anything the Antichrist can throw at us."

John nodded, squeezing her hand. "Together, we can face anything."

As they prepared for the days ahead, John and Emily drew strength from their shared resolve and their belief in the prophecies. They knew the fight against the Antichrist was just beginning, but they were ready to stand firm and fight for the truth.

And so, with the weight of their mission heavy on their shoulders, they prepared for the trials to come, determined to uncover the truth and stand as a beacon of hope in a world teetering on the edge of darkness.

The next morning dawned clear and bright, but John and Emily felt the weight of their task pressing heavily upon them. Their days were now consumed by studying, preparing, and reaching out to others who might offer support or knowledge.

John's phone buzzed with a message from Sarah. It was a photo of a flyer for a local community meeting that evening, discussing the recent global events. The flyer promised an open forum where people could share their experiences and theories. Seeing this, John decided it was crucial to attend. They needed to understand how the broader community was coping and whether there were others like them who were trying to piece together the truth.

That evening, John, Emily, and Pastor Williams arrived at the community center, where a crowd had gathered. The room was filled with a mix of anxious citizens, conspiracy theorists, and a few local leaders. The atmosphere was charged with a sense of urgency and confusion.

John and Emily took seats toward the back, observing the various discussions that were unfolding. The meeting began with a brief introduction from a local journalist, followed by open remarks from attendees.

One speaker, a middle-aged man with a graying beard, spoke passionately about the global disappearance. "It's all part of a massive conspiracy! The governments are hiding the truth from us. They want to control us, and they're using these disappearances to implement their agenda!"

The crowd murmured in agreement, but John felt uneasy. While skepticism was healthy, he feared that such theories might obscure the truth they were seeking.

Another speaker, a young woman in a worn-out hoodie, spoke more cautiously. "I've been trying to understand the spiritual side of this. My church has been discussing how this might be linked to biblical prophecies. If it's true, we need to prepare ourselves spiritually and physically."

John's interest was piqued. He saw an opportunity to connect with like-minded individuals. After the meeting, he approached the woman.

"Hi, I'm John Carter. I couldn't help but notice your comments. We've been studying the prophecies ourselves and have some insights we believe might be relevant. Do you mind if we talk?"

The woman, whose name was Rachel, agreed with a nod. They moved to a quieter corner of the room where Rachel explained that her church had been delving into prophetic texts and trying to make sense of the recent events. She was particularly interested in the concept of a coming "false peace" and the rise of a global leader, which aligned with what John had been uncovering.

As they spoke, John shared some of their findings, including the manuscript they had discovered and the insights Pastor Williams had provided. Rachel listened intently, her eyes widening as she connected the dots with her own research.

"This is exactly what we've been discussing," Rachel said. "If what you're saying is true, then we're in the midst of a significant prophetic event. But what do we do now?"

John felt a renewed sense of purpose. "We need to gather more people who understand these prophecies and prepare ourselves for the trials ahead. We also need to keep a close eye on the global developments and any signs of the Antichrist's rise."

Rachel nodded in agreement. "There's a small group of us who meet regularly to discuss these things. I'd be glad to introduce you to them. We've been trying to stay ahead of the misinformation and focus on the truth."

Later that week, John, Emily, and Pastor Williams met with Rachel and her group. The gathering took place in a dimly lit room, filled with worn-out chairs and makeshift tables covered in books and papers. The group was diverse, including theologians, scholars, and concerned citizens, all united by their quest for truth.

Rachel introduced John and Emily to the group, explaining their findings and the research they had conducted. The group welcomed them warmly, eager to share their own discoveries and collaborate on understanding the unfolding events.

During the discussion, a seasoned theologian named Dr. Jonathan Reid presented his own research. "We've been analyzing ancient texts and historical patterns. One thing that stands out is the idea of a 'false messiah' who will come with promises of peace but will ultimately bring destruction."

John's attention sharpened. "That's consistent with what we've found. The Antichrist will present himself as a savior, but his true nature will be revealed through his actions and the resulting chaos."

Dr. Reid nodded. "Exactly. We also need to be vigilant about signs and wonders. The Antichrist will perform miracles to deceive people, as prophesied in the Bible. We must be cautious and discerning."

Emily raised a crucial point. "How do we prepare for the mark of the beast? What steps can we take to ensure we don't fall into the trap of false allegiance?"

Dr. Reid responded thoughtfully. "The mark of the beast is a sign of allegiance to the Antichrist. We need to remain steadfast in our faith and find ways to support one another through the trials. Building a network of believers and staying informed will be key to resisting the Antichrist's influence."

As the meeting concluded, John felt a sense of solidarity and hope. The group's collective knowledge and determination provided a beacon of clarity amid the confusion. They had allies, and they were not alone in their quest for truth.

That night, as John and Emily prepared to leave, John reflected on the progress they had made. They had found valuable allies and gained deeper insights into the prophetic events. The path ahead was still fraught with uncertainty, but they had a clearer understanding of the challenges they would face.

As they drove home, John turned to Emily. "We've made significant strides, but there's much more to do. We need to stay vigilant and continue gathering information. The world is changing rapidly, and we must be prepared for whatever comes next."

Emily nodded, her expression resolute. "We'll face it together, John. We have our faith and our allies. That's our strength."

John smiled, feeling a renewed sense of purpose. With their newfound allies and a deeper understanding of the prophecies, they were better equipped to face the trials ahead. The journey was just beginning, and they were ready to confront the darkness with hope and determination.

As they settled into their routine, John and Emily remained committed to their mission. They continued to study, prepare, and connect with others, determined to uncover the truth and stand firm in their faith. The road ahead was uncertain, but they faced it with courage, knowing that their journey was part of a greater plan.

Chapter 6: The Antichrist Emerges

THE DAYS FOLLOWING their meeting with Rachel's group were marked by an uneasy calm. The world continued to reel from the aftershocks of the Rapture, but life in John Carter's small town had returned to a semblance of normalcy. As news of global chaos began to fade from the headlines, John and his family found themselves increasingly focused on understanding the larger forces at play.

One evening, as John sat at his kitchen table reviewing notes, Emily entered with a troubled expression. She handed John a newspaper, the headline catching his eye: "Charismatic Leader Emerges: A New Hope for a Divided World?"

John's heart raced. The article detailed the rise of a man named Alexander Voss, a former business mogul who had recently gained widespread popularity for his speeches on unity and peace. The article portrayed Voss as a beacon of hope, promising to restore order and bring stability to the world.

"I've been hearing his name a lot lately," Emily said, her voice tinged with concern. "It seems like everyone is rallying behind him."

John's mind raced as he thought of the prophecies he had studied. Voss's emergence seemed almost too perfectly timed, aligning with the biblical predictions about the Antichrist. John shared his thoughts with Emily, and they agreed it was crucial to investigate Voss further.

Over the next few days, John and Emily tracked Voss's public appearances and speeches. They noticed a recurring theme: Voss spoke of "a new world order" and "global peace," using terms that seemed to echo the prophecies of a false messiah. His rhetoric was smooth and persuasive, drawing people in with promises of a utopian future while subtly consolidating power.

One evening, Rachel contacted John with urgent news. "We've discovered some disturbing information about Voss. There are reports of him meeting with influential leaders and implementing policies that align with biblical warnings."

John and Emily joined Rachel at a local coffee shop where she shared her findings. Rachel had uncovered evidence suggesting that Voss was quietly negotiating with global leaders to centralize authority under his control. His proposals included establishing a global surveillance system and a universal identification system, both of which alarmingly mirrored descriptions of the mark of the beast.

"That's exactly what the prophecies warned about," Rachel said, her voice low. "He's positioning himself as the savior while laying the groundwork for total control."

John nodded, feeling a cold determination. "We need to gather more evidence and understand his plans better. If he's the Antichrist, we must act before it's too late."

The following week, John and Emily attended a public rally for Alexander Voss, hoping to witness firsthand the growing support and the leader's methods of persuasion. The rally was held in a massive stadium, filled with thousands of enthusiastic supporters. The atmosphere was electric, with banners proclaiming slogans like "Unity Through Strength" and "Peace for All."

As Voss took the stage, his presence was magnetic. He spoke with a commanding voice, promising to unite the fractured world through a new system of governance. His charisma and eloquence captivated the audience, making it clear why so many were drawn to him.

"Today, we stand at the dawn of a new era," Voss proclaimed, raising his arms to the crowd. "An era of prosperity and peace, where every person will have a place, and every nation will be part of a greater whole."

John and Emily observed the crowd's reaction with growing apprehension. The sheer force of Voss's personality and his ability to inspire hope was undeniable. However, John remained focused on the underlying message and the implications of his policies.

After the rally, John and Emily regrouped with Rachel and Pastor Williams. They discussed the need to expose Voss's true nature to the public and to prepare for the inevitable confrontation.

Rachel brought up an important point. "If Voss is the Antichrist, we need to be ready for the global impact of his rule. We must also be cautious of his influence over the media and governments."

Pastor Williams nodded in agreement. "We should continue our efforts to educate others and build a network of resistance. Our mission is to stay vigilant and offer a counter-narrative to the false promises."

As the days passed, John and his allies worked tirelessly to gather more information on Voss's activities and to spread awareness of the potential dangers. They continued to attend rallies, monitor news reports, and engage with other concerned citizens.

John's apprehension grew as Voss's influence expanded. The leader's policies began to take shape, including proposals for a universal biometric identification system and a global economic restructuring plan. These measures were sold as necessary for security and stability, but John and his allies saw them as steps toward a totalitarian regime.

One night, as John and Emily reviewed their notes, the weight of their mission felt heavier than ever. They knew that the struggle against the Antichrist would require more than just vigilance—it would require a united effort to resist and to stand firm in their faith.

"We're on the brink of something monumental," John said, his voice resolute. "The world is being reshaped before our eyes, and we need to be prepared for the battles ahead."

Emily reached out and squeezed his hand. "We'll face it together, John. With our allies and our faith, we can make a difference."

As they continued their preparations, John felt a deep sense of purpose. The emergence of Alexander Voss was only the beginning of a much larger conflict. But with their growing network and unwavering determination, John and his allies were ready to confront the challenges and fight for the truth.

The journey ahead was fraught with uncertainty, but they were committed to their mission. The rise of the Antichrist marked a turning point in their struggle, and they were prepared to face whatever lay ahead with courage and resolve.

THE WEEKS THAT FOLLOWED Voss's rally saw a rapid acceleration in his rise to power. His promises of a new world order began to take shape with alarming speed. Governments worldwide convened under his influence, and policies aligned with his vision were rapidly enacted. Voss's charisma and persuasive rhetoric had successfully bridged ideological divides, drawing in leaders and citizens alike with his vision of global unity and prosperity.

John and his team were increasingly troubled by the developments. Reports of Voss's growing control over media and communications were especially concerning. The media, once diverse in its coverage, now seemed to uniformly sing Voss's praises, broadcasting his speeches and policies as if they were gospel.

One evening, as John sat in his makeshift office, he received a call from Rachel. Her voice was urgent. "John, we've got a lead on something big. I need you to meet me at the library. It's about Voss's connections."

John arrived at the library to find Rachel already there, surrounded by a collection of documents and news clippings. She was joined by Pastor Williams and a few trusted members of their network.

"What's going on?" John asked, looking at the array of papers.

Rachel gestured to a large map pinned on the wall. "We've traced several key figures in Voss's inner circle. They're all connected to organizations and individuals with a history of political and financial manipulation. It's clear that Voss isn't just a charismatic leader; he's orchestrating a global takeover with a carefully planned agenda."

Pastor Williams leaned in, pointing to a series of documents. "These reports suggest that Voss is consolidating power through both overt and covert means. There are indications that he's implementing systems of control that align with the prophecies we've studied."

Rachel nodded. "We've also found evidence that Voss is planning to introduce a global identification system. It's being marketed as a way to ensure security and streamline services, but it's clear that it could be used for surveillance and control."

John's mind raced as he considered the implications. "If Voss is indeed the Antichrist, these measures could be the first steps toward implementing the mark of the beast."

Rachel looked at John with a mixture of determination and concern. "We need to expose this. The public must be made aware of what's really happening. But we have to be careful. Voss has a stranglehold on the media, and dissent is being swiftly suppressed."

Pastor Williams added, "We should focus on reaching out to local communities and small networks that are still independent of Voss's influence. They might be more receptive to our message."

As the meeting concluded, John felt a renewed sense of urgency. The task ahead was daunting, but the stakes were too high to ignore. He knew they needed to act quickly to counter Voss's influence and to protect those who were still unaware of the looming threat.

That night, John and Emily discussed their next steps. They decided to focus on gathering and disseminating information about Voss's activities and policies. Their goal was to build a network of informed citizens who could resist the impending changes and stand against the growing tide of tyranny.

The following days were a whirlwind of activity. John, Emily, and their allies worked tirelessly to distribute flyers, hold secret meetings, and leverage any remaining independent media sources. They faced numerous challenges, from government surveillance to hostile reactions from those loyal to Voss.

Despite the obstacles, John saw signs of hope. Small communities and groups began to respond to their efforts, showing solidarity and willingness to stand against Voss's agenda. These connections were crucial in building a broader resistance movement.

One evening, as John reviewed their progress, he received another call from Rachel. "John, I have some troubling news. There's a major summit being held where Voss is expected to announce a new global policy. This could be a pivotal moment."

John's heart sank. He knew that any major policy announcement could further consolidate Voss's power and accelerate the implementation of his agenda. "We need to get to that summit. If we can't attend in person, we should at least try to gather information and expose it."

Rachel agreed. "I'll do what I can to get a closer look. We need to be ready for whatever happens next."

The stage was set for a critical moment in the struggle against Voss's rise to power. John and his allies prepared for the upcoming summit, knowing that their actions could make a significant impact. The fight against the Antichrist was intensifying, and they were determined to stand firm in their mission to protect freedom and truth.

As John looked out at the night sky, he reflected on the journey that had brought him to this point. The road ahead was fraught with challenges, but he was resolute in his commitment. The emergence of Alexander Voss as a global power was a harbinger of the trials to come, and John and his team were ready to face them with unwavering resolve.

Chapter 7: The Resistance Forms

IN THE WEEKS FOLLOWING the summit, John and his allies focused on expanding their network and solidifying their resistance efforts. The announcement of Voss's new global policy had further consolidated his control, leading to widespread fears of a dystopian future. The need for organized resistance was more urgent than ever.

John convened a meeting at their makeshift headquarters, a rented warehouse on the outskirts of town. The room was filled with a mix of familiar faces and new recruits, all sharing a common goal: to stand against Voss's growing tyranny. The air was thick with determination and a palpable sense of camaraderie.

Rachel opened the meeting, her voice steady despite the gravity of the situation. "We've made some progress in spreading awareness, but Voss's influence is spreading faster than we anticipated. It's time to take our efforts to the next level. We need to formalize our resistance and create a coordinated strategy."

Pastor Williams nodded in agreement. "Our goal now is to establish cells across different regions, each working independently but in concert with the others. This way, we can maximize our impact while minimizing the risk of Voss's forces crushing us all at once."

John addressed the group, his gaze sweeping over the faces of those assembled. "We need to focus on several key areas: information dissemination, grassroots mobilization, and direct actions against Voss's infrastructure. We also need to secure our operations from infiltration and surveillance."

Several members of the group, including former military personnel and skilled activists, volunteered to take on specific roles. Some were tasked with gathering and analyzing intelligence, while others would focus on building local support networks and organizing protests. The planning was meticulous, reflecting the seriousness of their mission.

One of the new recruits, a tech-savvy young woman named Clara, spoke up. "I've been working on a secure communication network to help us coordinate. We'll need to stay one step ahead of Voss's surveillance if we're going to succeed."

John gave her a reassuring nod. "That's excellent. We'll need all the technological support we can get. Keep us updated on any developments."

As the meeting continued, the group discussed various strategies for undermining Voss's regime. They planned to leverage social media to expose Voss's actions, organize covert operations to disrupt his plans, and foster alliances with other dissenting groups. The sense of purpose was palpable, and for the first time, John felt a glimmer of hope amid the darkness.

Later that week, John and Rachel traveled to a nearby city to meet with representatives from several other resistance groups. The city had become a hub of activity for those opposed to Voss's regime, and John hoped to build a coalition that could present a united front against their common enemy.

The meeting took place in a discreet location, a small café with an unassuming exterior but a network of underground connections. The representatives included leaders from various backgrounds: former politicians, activists, and even disillusioned members of Voss's own administration.

John introduced himself and explained their group's goals. "We're looking to form a coalition to unite our efforts against Voss's regime. We believe that by working together, we can have a greater impact and better protect ourselves from Voss's increasing control."

The response was positive, with many leaders expressing their support and willingness to collaborate. However, there were also concerns about trust and coordination. Each group had its own methods and priorities, and integrating their efforts would require careful negotiation and compromise.

Over the next few days, John and Rachel worked tirelessly to establish agreements and coordinate strategies. They arranged for joint operations, shared intelligence, and set up secure communication channels. The coalition began to take shape, with each member group contributing its strengths to the collective effort.

One evening, as John returned to their headquarters, he was greeted by a sense of accomplishment and cautious optimism. The resistance was growing stronger, and their network was expanding. Yet, the challenges ahead remained daunting, and the threat posed by Voss's regime was ever-present.

John gathered his team for a briefing. "We've made significant progress in forming alliances and expanding our network. Our next steps involve executing coordinated actions to disrupt Voss's infrastructure and continue spreading awareness. We must stay vigilant and adaptable as the situation evolves."

Emily, who had been working on community outreach, added, "We've also seen increased support from local communities. People are beginning to question Voss's motives and are more open to joining our cause. We need to capitalize on this momentum."

John nodded, his resolve strengthened by the progress they had made. "We're building something important here, something that could make a real difference. Let's stay focused and keep pushing forward."

As the team dispersed to carry out their assignments, John took a moment to reflect on their journey. The formation of the resistance was a crucial step in the fight against Voss's tyranny. The road ahead would be fraught with danger and uncertainty, but John was determined to see it through. With the support of their allies and the strength of their convictions, they had a fighting chance to reclaim their freedom and stand against the encroaching darkness.

The resistance was taking shape, and the struggle against Voss's regime was only beginning.

As the resistance network expanded, John and his allies faced a series of escalating challenges. Voss's regime, ever vigilant and ruthless, responded to their activities with increasing force. Surveillance intensified, and targeted raids against suspected resistance members became more frequent.

One evening, while reviewing intelligence reports with Rachel and Clara, John received alarming news. A key contact in a neighboring city had been arrested during a raid. The contact had been instrumental in organizing local support and gathering critical information about Voss's operations.

"This is a serious blow," Rachel said, her face etched with concern. "Losing them could compromise our entire strategy in that region."

John nodded, his expression grim. "We need to act quickly to mitigate the damage. We should redirect our efforts and secure our remaining contacts. Clara, can you enhance our encryption protocols to ensure our communications are secure?"

Clara's fingers flew over her laptop as she worked to strengthen their communication network. "I'll make it a priority. We can't afford any more breaches."

John and Rachel discussed their next steps, weighing the risks of continuing with their current plans versus adjusting their strategy to avoid further losses. They decided to implement contingency measures, including the decentralization of some operations and increased security for sensitive communications.

Meanwhile, John's family remained a source of emotional strength and grounding for him. Emily had taken on the role of providing support to other families affected by the crisis. Her compassion and resilience offered a beacon of hope amid the turmoil.

One afternoon, as John visited a local community center where Emily was working, he found her talking with a group of concerned residents. The center had become a gathering point for those seeking solace and answers.

Emily greeted John with a weary but determined smile. "We've been helping people understand what's happening and providing support. It's amazing how many are ready to stand up against Voss's regime. The community's spirit is strong."

John took a deep breath, appreciating Emily's unwavering dedication. "That's exactly what we need right now. We must keep building this support network and ensuring that people remain united."

Back at the resistance headquarters, John and his team prepared for an upcoming coordinated operation. They planned to disrupt a major supply line that was crucial to Voss's enforcement apparatus. The operation required careful planning and precise execution to avoid detection and maximize impact.

As the night of the operation approached, the team gathered for a final briefing. John reviewed the mission objectives, the roles of each member, and the contingency plans in case of unexpected developments.

"Remember, our goal is to create a significant disruption without putting ourselves at unnecessary risk," John said, addressing the team. "We've worked hard to get to this point, and we need to execute this operation with precision and caution."

The team members nodded, their faces reflecting a mix of determination and apprehension. The operation would be a test of their capabilities and resolve.

At dusk, the team set out on their mission. They moved in small, covert groups to avoid drawing attention. John's group approached the target area, a heavily guarded supply depot located on the outskirts of the city. The depot was critical to Voss's control, and disrupting it could have a significant impact.

John and his team used a combination of stealth and tactical expertise to breach the perimeter. Clara had provided them with cutting-edge equipment to disable security systems and avoid detection. They worked swiftly, placing explosives at strategic locations to maximize damage.

As they prepared to leave, John glanced at his watch, timing their departure to coincide with the planned detonation. The tension was palpable as the countdown neared its end. Finally, the explosives were set off, sending a powerful shockwave through the depot.

The resulting explosion was massive, lighting up the night sky and creating chaos among the guards. John and his team moved quickly through the ensuing confusion, making their way to a safe extraction point.

Back at the headquarters, the team gathered to debrief and assess the operation's success. The explosion had indeed caused significant disruption, and initial reports indicated that the supply line had been severely impacted. The operation had also sent a clear message to Voss's regime: the resistance was capable and determined.

Despite the success, John was mindful of the risks involved. The explosion would undoubtedly provoke a harsher response from Voss's forces. They needed to remain vigilant and adapt to the evolving situation.

As the team disbanded for the night, John took a moment to reflect on their progress. The resistance was growing, and their efforts were beginning to make a tangible difference. However, the challenges ahead remained formidable. The struggle against Voss's regime was far from over, and the stakes continued to rise.

John knew that every victory came with a cost, and the path to freedom would be fraught with danger and sacrifice. But with each step, they moved closer to their goal of reclaiming their world from tyranny. The fight was far from finished, and the resistance's resolve would be tested in the days to come.

The operation's success was a morale booster for the resistance, but it also signaled a dangerous escalation. In the days following the attack on the supply depot, Voss's regime began a relentless crackdown on suspected resistance cells. Curfews were enforced more strictly, and public executions of perceived enemies became a grim spectacle designed to instill fear.

John's team met frequently to strategize their next moves. The network of resistance cells had grown rapidly, thanks to their previous successes and increased public support. However, maintaining cohesion and security among the cells was becoming increasingly complex.

One evening, John convened a meeting with the leaders of the various cells. The meeting took place in a dimly lit underground bunker, designed to shield them from surveillance. Rachel, Clara, and other key members from different regions were present.

"We've made significant progress," John began, "but the regime's response has been severe. We need to adapt our strategy to keep our operations effective and our people safe."

Rachel, who had been working closely with several cells, spoke up. "We're seeing a lot of movement among local groups. People are eager to join the fight, but they lack proper training and coordination. We need to provide them with more structure and resources."

John nodded. "That's a crucial point. We need to ensure that new recruits are properly trained and integrated into our network without compromising our security. Clara, can you oversee the development of a standardized training program for new members?"

Clara agreed, already formulating ideas on how to implement the training efficiently while minimizing risks. "I'll get started on that right away. We need to balance speed with thoroughness to ensure effectiveness."

John turned to the other leaders. "We also need to strengthen our intelligence network. The regime's crackdown is likely to increase, and we need to stay ahead of their moves. I want each cell to establish secure communication channels and share intelligence regularly."

The room buzzed with agreement as the leaders began discussing their roles and responsibilities. Each leader was assigned specific tasks to ensure the smooth functioning of their cells and the overall coordination of the resistance efforts.

Meanwhile, Voss's regime intensified its efforts to quash the rebellion. Surveillance drones patrolled the skies, and informants were embedded within communities, making it increasingly difficult for the resistance to operate undetected. The regime's propaganda machine worked overtime, painting the resistance as a dangerous, chaotic force and attempting to turn public opinion against them.

Despite the oppressive atmosphere, John observed a growing determination among the people. Acts of defiance, from covert pamphleteering to public protests, became more frequent. The resistance was not only fighting a regime but also igniting a spark of hope among the oppressed.

One night, John and his team planned a covert operation to sabotage one of Voss's key propaganda centers. The center was responsible for spreading disinformation and propaganda designed to manipulate public perception and suppress dissent.

John's team infiltrated the center under the cover of darkness. Using the training and equipment provided by Clara, they navigated through the security systems and planted explosives in critical locations. Their goal was to create a significant disruption without causing unnecessary harm to innocent employees who might be unaware of the center's true purpose.

As they completed their task and prepared to leave, John reflected on the broader implications of their actions. The resistance's efforts were not just about striking at the regime but also about inspiring hope and resilience in a world dominated by fear.

The next morning, news of the sabotage spread quickly. The propaganda center was in ruins, and Voss's regime issued a statement condemning the attack and vowing retribution. The public's response was mixed, with some expressing anger and others showing support for the resistance's courage.

John and his team regrouped to assess the impact of the operation and plan their next steps. The attack had achieved its goal of disrupting the regime's propaganda efforts, but it also drew increased scrutiny and retaliation.

"The regime will likely intensify their crackdown," Rachel said as they reviewed the latest intelligence reports. "We need to be prepared for their response and adapt our tactics accordingly."

John agreed. "We've made significant strides, but the fight is far from over. Our success depends on our ability to stay united and agile. We must remain vigilant and continue to inspire hope in those who have lost faith."

As the resistance continued to grow and evolve, John and his allies faced new challenges and opportunities. The struggle against Voss's regime was a complex and perilous endeavor, but each victory, each act of defiance, brought them one step closer to reclaiming their world from tyranny. The road ahead would be fraught with danger, but the resistance was determined to persevere, driven by the belief that their fight for freedom was just beginning.

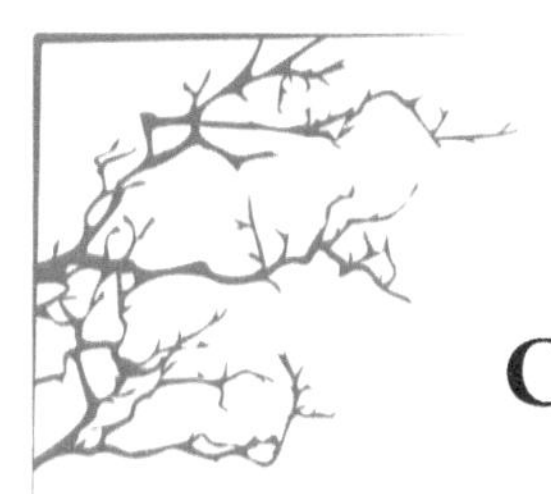

Chapter 8: The Moral Dilemma

JOHN CARTER'S DAYS were increasingly filled with strategic meetings, clandestine operations, and the ceaseless challenge of staying one step ahead of the regime. Yet, beneath the surface of their resistance efforts, a storm was brewing within their ranks—a storm of ethical and moral dilemmas that threatened to fracture their unity.

The resistance had become a formidable force, but as their activities grew bolder, the line between right and wrong began to blur. The cost of their struggle weighed heavily on everyone involved, and the consequences of their actions were becoming more apparent.

One evening, John called a meeting of his core team to discuss their latest operations and address some troubling issues that had arisen. The team gathered in the dimly lit safe house, their faces etched with fatigue and determination.

"We need to talk about the recent developments," John said, his voice grave. "Our actions have had significant impacts, both on our enemies and on innocent people caught in the crossfire. We need to address some tough questions about what we're doing and why."

Rachel, the tactical expert, was the first to speak. "We've had reports of increased civilian casualties from our recent operations. Our sabotage missions, while aimed at disrupting the regime, have sometimes affected people who had no part in our struggle."

Clara, who had been working on training and recruitment, nodded. "I've also heard concerns from new recruits. They're worried about the ethical implications of our actions and the possibility of collateral damage."

John sighed. "These are valid concerns. We have to balance our fight against the regime with the need to protect innocent lives. It's becoming increasingly difficult to draw a clear line between combatants and non-combatants."

The room was filled with a tense silence as the team grappled with these issues. The principles that had once guided their actions now seemed to conflict with the harsh realities of their resistance.

Emily, John's wife, who had been quietly observing the discussion, spoke up. "We can't lose sight of why we're fighting. We started this because we believed in justice and protecting those who can't protect themselves. If we compromise our principles, we risk becoming just like the regime we're fighting against."

John looked around at his team, seeing the weariness and doubt in their eyes. "We need to establish clearer guidelines for our operations. We must ensure that our actions are as precise and ethical as possible, and that we minimize harm to civilians. This might mean revising our strategies and re-evaluating our goals."

The discussion continued late into the night, as the team debated various approaches to ensure their operations remained morally justifiable. They discussed the need for better intelligence, more rigorous planning, and methods to verify targets to prevent civilian casualties.

Despite their best efforts, some decisions still weighed heavily on them. In a world where survival often came at a high cost, maintaining a moral compass was increasingly challenging.

As the meeting concluded, John felt a renewed sense of responsibility. The resistance was more than just a military struggle; it was a fight for the soul of their movement. The principles they upheld were as crucial as their tactical successes.

In the following days, the resistance implemented new protocols designed to address the ethical concerns raised by the team. They enhanced their intelligence-gathering efforts to ensure precision in their operations and provided additional training to their members on the importance of minimizing harm.

Despite these measures, the internal tensions continued. The moral dilemmas faced by the resistance began to strain relationships within their ranks. Members who had once been united by a common cause now found themselves divided by differing views on the means and ends of their struggle.

John and his core team faced the difficult task of navigating these challenges while maintaining their focus on the broader goal of toppling Voss's regime. They continued to fight for justice, but they also worked to heal the fractures within their movement, striving to uphold their values in the face of overwhelming adversity.

As the resistance pressed forward, the stakes grew ever higher. The struggle for freedom was not just a battle against an oppressive regime but also a quest to preserve the ideals that had inspired their fight. Each decision, each action, was a step along a precarious path, fraught with moral and ethical challenges that would test their resolve and define their legacy.

John Carter's thoughts were troubled as he left the safe house. The weight of the moral and ethical issues they faced seemed heavier than ever. As he walked through the dimly lit streets, his mind replayed the discussions from the meeting, struggling to reconcile their principles with the harsh realities of their fight.

The city had become a battleground of ideologies as much as a physical space. People whispered about the resistance, and the regime's propaganda twisted truths and amplified fears. John's resolve was tested by the knowledge that every action they took rippled through the community in ways they couldn't always predict.

As he reached home, he found Emily waiting for him in the small kitchen. The flickering light from the overhead lamp cast a warm glow over her face, a stark contrast to the cold reality John had been grappling with.

"How did the meeting go?" she asked softly, noticing his troubled expression.

"It was intense," John replied, sinking into a chair. "We talked about the impact of our operations on civilians and the ethical challenges we're facing. It's clear we need to do more to minimize harm, but it's not an easy task."

Emily nodded thoughtfully. "I've seen the toll it's taking on everyone. The resistance is made up of people who care deeply about this cause. They're trying to do the right thing, but sometimes the lines get blurred."

John sighed, running a hand through his hair. "I know. We're in a tough spot. We need to be vigilant about not becoming what we're fighting against. It's a delicate balance, and it's wearing us down."

Emily reached out, placing a comforting hand on his. "You're doing the best you can. Sometimes, we have to make difficult decisions and live with the consequences. But it's important to stay true to our values, even in the darkest times."

John appreciated her support but knew that words alone wouldn't resolve the underlying issues. The resistance's recent actions had left a trail of discontent and uncertainty among its members. They needed a way to address the internal discord and reinforce their commitment to their moral code.

The next day, John convened another meeting with the core team to implement some of the new guidelines they had discussed. He wanted to ensure that the principles they had agreed upon were put into practice.

"Today, we're going to focus on refining our strategies and improving our protocols," John began. "We need to make sure that our actions are as precise as possible and that we are minimizing harm to innocent civilians. This isn't just about military success; it's about maintaining our integrity."

Rachel presented the updated operational guidelines, which included stricter protocols for verifying targets and more detailed planning to reduce collateral damage. Clara and the others discussed new training programs for resistance members to reinforce the importance of ethical conduct.

Despite their efforts, it was evident that not everyone was fully onboard. Some members of the resistance felt that the new guidelines would hamper their effectiveness and limit their ability to strike at the regime's core. Tensions were high as differing opinions clashed.

During one particularly heated debate, Marcus, a seasoned operative, expressed his frustration. "We're fighting a ruthless regime. Sometimes, tough measures are necessary to achieve our goals. We can't afford to be paralyzed by moral dilemmas when lives are at stake."

John countered, "I understand your frustration, Marcus, but if we lose sight of our principles, we risk becoming just another oppressive force. We need to find a way to fight effectively without compromising our values."

The discussion revealed a deep divide within the resistance. While some members embraced the new ethical guidelines, others questioned whether they would be effective in the face of the regime's brutality. The disagreement underscored the complexity of their situation and the challenges of maintaining unity in the midst of an ongoing struggle.

In the weeks that followed, John and his team worked tirelessly to address the discord within the resistance. They facilitated more open dialogues, encouraged feedback, and sought to reconcile differing viewpoints. The goal was to forge a cohesive strategy that balanced military objectives with ethical considerations.

Despite their efforts, the resistance faced increasing pressure from the regime's relentless countermeasures. The regime's forces intensified their crackdowns, and the city's atmosphere grew more oppressive. As the situation became more dire, the stakes continued to rise.

John and his team pressed on, driven by a renewed sense of purpose. They understood that their struggle was not just about overthrowing the regime but also about preserving their humanity in the process. The moral dilemmas they faced were a constant reminder of the fine line they walked between justice and vengeance.

As John prepared for a critical night operation, he couldn't shake the mounting pressure. The upcoming raid on a regime facility promised to be a significant blow to their adversaries but also carried substantial risk to civilian lives. The recent debate over ethics weighed heavily on him, and he was determined to ensure the mission aligned with their new protocols.

The team gathered in the briefing room, where Clara laid out the operation details. "This facility is a key communications hub for the regime. Disabling it will disrupt their control and communication capabilities, giving us a strategic advantage," Clara explained. "We've taken every precaution to avoid civilian areas and limit collateral damage."

John nodded, but he could see the tension in his team's faces. They all knew the stakes but also recognized the fine line between effective resistance and moral compromise.

Rachel, who had been instrumental in refining their operational guidelines, addressed the group. "We've mapped out multiple routes to ensure we minimize risk. Every step has been planned with precision. But remember, we must remain vigilant and adaptable. If the situation changes, we need to reassess immediately."

John appreciated her focus but felt a gnawing doubt. The regime's response to their activities had grown more severe, and the city's growing resentment was palpable. It wasn't just their safety on the line; the moral implications of their actions were becoming increasingly significant.

"Everyone, let's stay sharp tonight," John said, trying to inject confidence into his voice. "We're here not just to fight the regime but to uphold our principles. Remember why we're doing this and the values we're defending."

As night fell, the team prepared to move out. They slipped through the darkened streets, avoiding heavily patrolled areas. The tension was thick, but their training and determination kept them focused. They reached the outskirts of the facility, a fortress of steel and concrete that loomed ominously against the night sky.

John, Clara, and a small squad moved in, each member adhering to their assigned roles. They set up perimeter defenses and began disabling the security systems. Everything was proceeding as planned until an unexpected complication arose: a patrol had been rerouted, and a group of civilians, presumably working late or trying to flee, found themselves in the line of fire.

John's heart raced as he watched through the scope of his rifle. The civilians were dangerously close to the operation's target area. The initial plan had not accounted for this new development, and the team faced a critical decision. They could push forward with the mission, risking civilian casualties, or pull back and reassess, potentially losing the element of surprise and jeopardizing the entire operation.

The debate was swift and heated. Clara advocated for pulling back, emphasizing their commitment to minimizing harm. Marcus, however, was impatient and argued for proceeding to ensure the regime's communication hub was disabled. "We've come too far to back out now," he said. "If we don't act, the regime will tighten its grip even further."

John was torn. He could see the validity in both arguments but knew that any decision would carry consequences. He looked at his team, the faces illuminated by the faint light of their equipment, and made a decision.

"We pull back," John said firmly. "The civilians are our priority. We'll need to regroup and come up with a new plan."

The team quickly executed a retreat, managing to avoid detection as they withdrew. John's mind was racing as they regrouped at the safe house. The mission had been a partial failure, but he hoped they had done the right thing by prioritizing the safety of innocent lives.

Back at the safe house, tensions were high. The team debriefed, and the mood was somber. Marcus and a few others expressed frustration over the missed opportunity. "We had a chance to strike a blow against the regime, and we hesitated," he said bitterly.

John faced the team, his own frustration evident. "This isn't just about striking blows. It's about what we stand for. If we lose our moral compass, we risk becoming the very thing we're fighting against. We need to find a balance between effective action and ethical conduct."

Rachel spoke up, offering some perspective. "We did what we believed was right. We have to be prepared for the fact that not every mission will go as planned. But if we maintain our principles, we'll preserve our integrity, and that matters in the long run."

The team members slowly nodded, recognizing the truth in her words. The mission's failure was a setback, but it reinforced their commitment to their ethical guidelines.

As dawn approached, John felt the weight of their decisions pressing down on him. The battle was far from over, and the path ahead was fraught with challenges. But he remained resolute in his belief that their fight was not just against the regime but also against the erosion of their values.

The chapter closed with the team readying for the next phase of their struggle. They had faced a moral dilemma and emerged with renewed determination to navigate the complexities of their fight while holding onto their core beliefs.

Chapter 9: The Turning Point

JOHN AWOKE TO THE SOUND of distant sirens, their wails a stark reminder of the growing chaos outside. The news had been grim: the regime had intensified its crackdown, and reports of escalating disasters were becoming commonplace. His mind was heavy with the events of the previous night and the unresolved issues plaguing their efforts.

He joined the team in the dimly lit common room, where Clara was pouring over intelligence reports. Her face was drawn, reflecting the strain of their recent setbacks.

"Morning," John greeted, trying to mask his own fatigue. "What's the situation?"

Clara glanced up. "It's worse than we thought. The regime has implemented stricter controls, and there are rumors of increased brutality. We've also got reports of strange phenomena—earthquakes, sudden storms. Some say these are signs of something more sinister."

John's heart sank. He had hoped for some respite, but the news only confirmed his fears. "What about our next steps? Do we have any leads?"

Rachel, who had been studying satellite images, spoke up. "There's a pattern emerging. The regime's recent actions seem to be coordinated with the disasters. It's almost like they're using these events to consolidate their power further."

Marcus, who had joined them, nodded. "We need to find out if there's a connection. If they're behind these disasters or if it's something else entirely, it could change everything."

John agreed. "Let's split up. Clara, you and Rachel investigate the regime's activities and try to find any links to the disasters. Marcus and I will follow up on reports of resistance movements and see if they have any information."

The team dispersed, each heading towards their respective tasks. John and Marcus visited several resistance cells, gathering intel and assessing the situation. The atmosphere in the underground meetings was tense; the fear of the regime's growing power was palpable, and rumors of a mysterious figure behind the chaos began to circulate.

During one such meeting, an informant named Leo provided a critical piece of information. "There's talk of a high-ranking official within the regime who's been seen at the epicenters of these disasters," Leo said, his voice low and urgent. "People are calling him the 'Harbinger.' They say he's using these events to push forward a hidden agenda."

John's curiosity was piqued. "Do you have any idea who this Harbinger is or what their goals might be?"

Leo shook his head. "Not much. Only that he's a key player and seems to have access to resources and knowledge beyond ordinary means."

As John and Marcus left the meeting, they discussed the implications. "If this Harbinger is connected to the regime and the disasters, we might be looking at something much bigger than we anticipated," Marcus said.

John nodded. "We need to get this information to the team and see what we can uncover. This might be the breakthrough we need."

Back at the safe house, the team reconvened. Clara and Rachel had made progress in their investigation. "We've found evidence linking the regime's operations to the areas hit by the disasters," Clara reported. "It seems like there's a deliberate effort to manipulate these events to maintain control."

Rachel added, "We also discovered something intriguing. There's a secret project within the regime focused on harnessing or predicting these disasters. It's still unclear, but it might be related to the Harbinger."

John's mind raced. The pieces were beginning to fit together, but the full picture remained elusive. "We need to get more concrete evidence. If this Harbinger is as influential as we think, finding and exposing them could turn the tide."

The team agreed to focus their efforts on uncovering the identity and objectives of the Harbinger. They planned a series of covert operations to infiltrate key regime facilities and gather additional intelligence. As they prepared for the next phase, John felt a renewed sense of urgency.

The discovery of the Harbinger and their connection to the regime's machinations provided a glimmer of hope amidst the growing darkness. With their resolve hardened and their focus sharpened, John and his allies faced the impending confrontation with a newfound determination to unveil the truth and fight for their cause.

As the team prepared for their mission, the atmosphere in the safe house was electric with tension and determination. The stakes had never been higher, and everyone understood the gravity of their task. John, Marcus, Clara, and Rachel gathered around a table strewn with maps and documents, strategizing their next move.

"We've identified three key locations where the Harbinger might be operating," Clara began, pointing to various spots on the map. "The first is a research facility in the outskirts of the city, rumored to be involved in disaster prediction. The second is a high-security data center where the regime stores sensitive information. The third is a government building where we've heard the Harbinger has been making frequent visits."

John studied the map carefully. "We need to prioritize these locations based on their potential for yielding useful information. I suggest we start with the research facility. If the Harbinger is involved in predicting disasters, it's likely they're also experimenting with ways to control or escalate them."

The team nodded in agreement. "We'll need to gather intel on the facility's security measures and create a plan for infiltration," Marcus said. "I'll take charge of that."

Rachel chimed in, "I can work on decrypting any communications or data we might recover from the facility. We need to understand what kind of technology or research they're using."

Clara offered to coordinate logistics and support, ensuring the team had the necessary equipment and safe routes. "I'll also set up a secure channel for communication during the operation. We need to stay connected and be ready for any unforeseen complications."

As the team split up to tackle their respective tasks, John couldn't shake the feeling that they were on the verge of something significant. The information about the Harbinger and the regime's disaster projects had injected a sense of urgency into their mission. If they could uncover the truth, they might not only expose the regime's dark plans but also find a way to stop them.

John and Marcus spent the afternoon surveying the research facility from a safe distance. The facility was surrounded by high fences, patrolled by guards, and monitored by security cameras. It was clear that the regime took its operations seriously.

"We'll need to approach this carefully," John said, his eyes scanning the perimeter. "We'll need a distraction to get past the initial security, and once inside, we'll have to move quickly."

Marcus nodded. "I'll work on creating a diversion. If we can draw the guards away from the main entrance, we should be able to slip in through a service door. From there, we'll need to find the central lab or data storage area."

As night fell, the team executed their plan. Marcus created a distraction by setting off a small, controlled explosion away from the facility. The guards, alerted by the commotion, rushed to investigate. Seizing the opportunity, John and Marcus slipped through the service entrance.

Inside, the facility was eerily quiet. The hum of machinery and the occasional beeping of computers provided the only sounds. The two men navigated through a series of hallways, guided by Clara's map and Rachel's intel.

After several tense moments, they reached the central lab. The room was filled with sophisticated equipment and stacks of documents. John and Marcus quickly set to work, searching for any information related to the Harbinger or the regime's disaster projects.

John found a locked cabinet containing several folders marked with ominous labels such as "Project Harbinger" and "Disaster Manipulation." He used the tools they had brought to break the lock and retrieve the files. Marcus downloaded data from several computer terminals, ensuring they had a complete set of information.

Just as they were about to leave, an unexpected noise echoed through the facility—footsteps approaching fast. "We've been compromised!" Marcus hissed, grabbing the files. "We need to get out of here, now!"

The two men made a hasty retreat, retracing their steps through the facility. They managed to evade capture by using the shadows and narrow corridors, eventually making their way back to the service entrance.

As they emerged into the night, John's mind raced with the implications of their findings. The files they had recovered were filled with detailed research on disaster prediction and manipulation, as well as disturbing evidence of the regime's plans to use these technologies for control.

Back at the safe house, the team gathered to review the documents. Clara and Rachel worked diligently to analyze the data, while John and Marcus briefed them on the operation.

"This is it," Rachel said, her voice filled with awe and concern. "The regime is not just predicting disasters—they're actively manipulating them. And the Harbinger... it looks like they're at the center of this."

John nodded. "We need to prepare for the next phase. The information we've gathered could be crucial in exposing the regime's plans and countering their efforts. But we also need to be ready for a direct confrontation with the Harbinger and the regime's forces."

The team's resolve was stronger than ever. The knowledge they had gained marked a turning point in their struggle, providing both hope and direction. As they prepared for the next steps in their fight against the regime, John felt a renewed sense of purpose..

The safe house buzzed with activity as the team gathered to debrief and strategize. The data they had recovered from the research facility revealed a grim reality. The regime's manipulation of natural disasters was far more advanced and insidious than anyone had imagined. The Harbinger, a shadowy figure linked to these experiments, was not just a mythical threat but a real, powerful force with dire plans.

John sat at the center of the room, a stack of documents and electronic files spread out before him. The team members were busy analyzing the information, their faces etched with worry and determination.

Rachel looked up from her computer, her eyes wide with concern. "The research shows that the regime plans to trigger a series of catastrophic events across multiple regions to consolidate their power further. They've developed a technology that can amplify natural disasters and create false crises."

Clara, who had been coordinating the analysis, nodded gravely. "We've also uncovered evidence that the Harbinger has been orchestrating these events behind the scenes. Their goal seems to be creating chaos and fear to weaken resistance and tighten their grip on power."

Marcus, who had been reviewing satellite images and security footage, interjected. "There's more. We've identified several key locations where these disasters are likely to be triggered. The Harbinger is coordinating with the regime's top officials to ensure maximum impact."

John's mind raced. The implications of their findings were enormous. If they could prevent or mitigate these disasters, they might be able to turn the tide in their favor. But it was clear that they needed to act quickly and decisively.

"We need to disrupt the Harbinger's plans before they can execute them," John said, his voice firm. "We've pinpointed the locations where the regime is preparing for these disasters. Our priority must be to sabotage their operations and gather more intelligence on their next move."

The team quickly mobilized. Clara and Rachel worked on pinpointing the exact timing and nature of the impending disasters using the data they had. Marcus and John planned a series of covert operations to disrupt the regime's preparations and gather additional evidence.

Their first target was a facility near the coast, where the regime was preparing to initiate a massive storm system. The team set out under the cover of darkness, using disguises and stealth tactics to approach the facility. The air was tense with anticipation as they moved through the shadows, avoiding security patrols and surveillance cameras.

Inside the facility, John and Marcus encountered a series of high-tech controls and monitoring systems. Their objective was to disable the equipment and prevent the activation of the storm system. Rachel and Clara, stationed outside, provided support and relayed critical information.

As they worked to dismantle the equipment, alarms suddenly blared throughout the facility. "We've been spotted!" Clara's voice crackled over the communication line. "You need to finish quickly and get out of there!"

John and Marcus worked with renewed urgency. They managed to disable the core components of the system just as security forces closed in. With the equipment rendered inoperable, the team made a hasty escape, narrowly avoiding capture.

Back at the safe house, the team regrouped and assessed the results of their operation. "We've successfully disrupted the storm system," Marcus reported, breathing heavily. "But the Harbinger's network is vast. We need to keep hitting their operations and gathering as much intel as possible."

Rachel reviewed the data they had retrieved from the facility. "This is just one piece of the puzzle. We still need to understand the full scope of the Harbinger's plans and how they're coordinating with the regime."

John nodded, determined. "We've made progress, but the real test will be uncovering the Harbinger's ultimate objective. We need to stay ahead of their plans and continue exposing their schemes."

The team's spirits were lifted by their success, but the gravity of their mission weighed heavily on them. The regime's reach was extensive, and the threat posed by the Harbinger was far from over. The resistance had gained a critical advantage, but they were entering a new phase of their struggle.

As they prepared for the next phase of their campaign, John felt a sense of both urgency and resolve. The battle against the regime and the Harbinger was far from over, but the team's determination and their recent victories gave them hope. The turning point had arrived, and with it, the promise of a potential breakthrough in their fight for freedom.

As the team prepared for their mission, the atmosphere in the safe house was electric with tension and determination. The stakes had never been higher, and everyone understood the gravity of their task. John, Marcus, Clara, and Rachel gathered around a table strewn with maps and documents, strategizing their next move.

"We've identified three key locations where the Harbinger might be operating," Clara began, pointing to various spots on the map. "The first is a research facility in the outskirts of the city, rumored to be involved in disaster prediction. The second is a high-security data center where the regime stores sensitive information. The third is a government building where we've heard the Harbinger has been making frequent visits."

John studied the map carefully. "We need to prioritize these locations based on their potential for yielding useful information. I suggest we start with the research facility. If the Harbinger is involved in predicting disasters, it's likely they're also experimenting with ways to control or escalate them."

The team nodded in agreement. "We'll need to gather intel on the facility's security measures and create a plan for infiltration," Marcus said. "I'll take charge of that."

Rachel chimed in, "I can work on decrypting any communications or data we might recover from the facility. We need to understand what kind of technology or research they're using."

Clara offered to coordinate logistics and support, ensuring the team had the necessary equipment and safe routes. "I'll also set up a secure channel for communication during the operation. We need to stay connected and be ready for any unforeseen complications."

As the team split up to tackle their respective tasks, John couldn't shake the feeling that they were on the verge of something significant. The information about the Harbinger and the regime's disaster projects had injected a sense of urgency into their mission. If they could uncover the truth, they might not only expose the regime's dark plans but also find a way to stop them.

John and Marcus spent the afternoon surveying the research facility from a safe distance. The facility was surrounded by high fences, patrolled by guards, and monitored by security cameras. It was clear that the regime took its operations seriously.

"We'll need to approach this carefully," John said, his eyes scanning the perimeter. "We'll need a distraction to get past the initial security, and once inside, we'll have to move quickly."

Marcus nodded. "I'll work on creating a diversion. If we can draw the guards away from the main entrance, we should be able to slip in through a service door. From there, we'll need to find the central lab or data storage area."

As night fell, the team executed their plan. Marcus created a distraction by setting off a small, controlled explosion away from the facility. The guards, alerted by the commotion, rushed to investigate. Seizing the opportunity, John and Marcus slipped through the service entrance.

Inside, the facility was eerily quiet. The hum of machinery and the occasional beeping of computers provided the only sounds. The two men navigated through a series of hallways, guided by Clara's map and Rachel's intel.

After several tense moments, they reached the central lab. The room was filled with sophisticated equipment and stacks of documents. John and Marcus quickly set to work, searching for any information related to the Harbinger or the regime's disaster projects.

John found a locked cabinet containing several folders marked with ominous labels such as "Project Harbinger" and "Disaster Manipulation." He used the tools they had brought to break the lock and retrieve the files. Marcus downloaded data from several computer terminals, ensuring they had a complete set of information.

Just as they were about to leave, an unexpected noise echoed through the facility—footsteps approaching fast. "We've been compromised!" Marcus hissed, grabbing the files. "We need to get out of here, now!"

The two men made a hasty retreat, retracing their steps through the facility. They managed to evade capture by using the shadows and narrow corridors, eventually making their way back to the service entrance.

As they emerged into the night, John's mind raced with the implications of their findings. The files they had recovered were filled with detailed research on disaster prediction and manipulation, as well as disturbing evidence of the regime's plans to use these technologies for control.

Back at the safe house, the team gathered to review the documents. Clara and Rachel worked diligently to analyze the data, while John and Marcus briefed them on the operation.

"This is it," Rachel said, her voice filled with awe and concern. "The regime is not just predicting disasters—they're actively manipulating them. And the Harbinger... it looks like they're at the center of this."

John nodded. "We need to prepare for the next phase. The information we've gathered could be crucial in exposing the regime's plans and countering their efforts. But we also need to be ready for a direct confrontation with the Harbinger and the regime's forces."

The team's resolve was stronger than ever. The knowledge they had gained marked a turning point in their struggle, providing both hope and direction. As they prepared for the next steps in their fight against the regime, John felt a renewed sense of purpose.

The chapter ended with the team facing the dawning realization that their battle was far from over. The discovery of the Harbinger's connection to the regime's sinister plans set the stage for an epic confrontation and deepened their commitment to uncovering the truth and fighting for their cause.

Chapter 10: The New Dawn

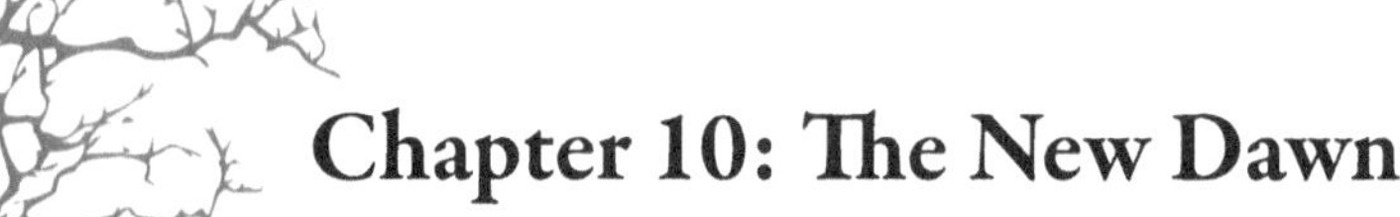

THE FIRST LIGHT OF dawn crept through the windows of the safe house, casting a soft glow over the room. The early morning calm belied the intensity of the previous night's events. John Carter and his team had made significant strides in their fight against the regime and the Harbinger, but the road ahead was still fraught with uncertainty.

John sat at the table, poring over the latest intelligence reports and reflecting on their recent victories. Despite their successes, the challenges they faced were immense. The Harbinger's influence was still pervasive, and the regime's control had tightened in many areas. Yet, there was a palpable shift in the atmosphere—a sense that they were on the cusp of a critical breakthrough.

Clara, Rachel, and Marcus gathered around the table, their expressions a mix of fatigue and determination. The previous night's operations had provided crucial insights into the Harbinger's next moves, and the team was ready to formulate their next plan of action.

"We've made progress," John began, breaking the silence. "Disrupting the storm system was a significant win, but it's only one part of a much larger puzzle. We need to continue exposing the Harbinger's plans and rallying support."

Rachel nodded in agreement. "We've identified several other key facilities and operations. Our next steps involve targeting these locations to prevent further disasters and weaken their control."

Marcus looked at the map spread out before them. "The Harbinger's network is extensive. We need to prioritize our targets and focus on disrupting their most critical operations."

As the team discussed their strategy, a sense of renewed purpose filled the room. They had weathered numerous challenges and had taken significant risks, but their efforts were beginning to pay off. The fight was far from over, but they were making headway.

Meanwhile, outside the safe house, the world was beginning to show signs of change. The resistance's efforts had started to inspire hope in communities across the globe. Small victories were being celebrated, and people were slowly beginning to rally against the regime's oppressive measures.

John's phone buzzed with an incoming message. He glanced at the screen and saw a message from one of their informants. The information was significant—new evidence about the Harbinger's ultimate plan and a potential weakness in their operations.

"We've received new intel," John said, showing the message to the team. "This could be the breakthrough we need. It seems the Harbinger has a critical vulnerability that we can exploit."

Clara's eyes brightened. "If we can target this weakness, we might be able to destabilize their operations and gain a significant advantage."

The team quickly formulated a plan based on the new information. They would launch a coordinated operation to strike at the heart of the Harbinger's operations, aiming to cripple their ability to manipulate and control global events.

As they prepared for the mission, John took a moment to reflect on their journey. The path had been fraught with danger and uncertainty, but the resilience and courage of the team had been unwavering. They had come a long way from their initial struggles, and their efforts were beginning to turn the tide in their favor.

The operation commenced with precision and determination. The team executed their plan flawlessly, disrupting key operations and exposing critical vulnerabilities in the Harbinger's network. The results were immediate—chaos erupted within the Harbinger's ranks, and their control over global events began to wane.

As the dust settled from the operation, the team gathered to assess the results. The impact of their actions was clear—the Harbinger's influence had been significantly weakened, and the regime's control had been challenged. The resistance had achieved a crucial victory, but they knew that their fight was far from over.

John stood before the team, his expression resolute. "We've made a significant impact, but there's still much work to be done. The Harbinger and the regime will not be easily defeated, and the world remains in turmoil. Our mission is far from complete, but we've taken a crucial step toward a better future."

The team nodded in agreement, their spirits lifted by their recent success. The battle against the Harbinger and the regime was far from over, but the progress they had made gave them hope for the future.

As the sun rose higher in the sky, the team prepared for the next phase of their struggle. The world was changing, and the resistance was at the forefront of that change. With renewed determination, they set out to continue their fight, knowing that their efforts were making a difference.

The chapter ended with a sense of cautious optimism. The resistance had achieved a significant victory, but the path ahead remained uncertain. The struggle against the Harbinger and the regime would continue, but the team was ready to face the challenges ahead with unwavering resolve. The dawn of a new era had begun, and the fight for freedom and justice would go on.

As the team regrouped and prepared for the next phase of their operations, the global situation continued to evolve. The Harbinger's network had been significantly disrupted, but the regime's resilience was evident. Communities around the world were beginning to recover from the immediate impact of the recent upheavals, and new alliances were forming among those who sought to rebuild and resist.

John and his team had set up a temporary command center in a remote location, away from the prying eyes of the regime. The room was filled with maps, reports, and communication equipment. The team members worked diligently, analyzing the results of their latest operation and planning their next steps.

Clara, working alongside Rachel, sifted through intelligence reports. "We've received reports of increased resistance activity in several key areas," Clara noted. "It seems like our efforts have inspired others to join the fight."

Rachel nodded, her eyes focused on the screen. "We need to coordinate with these new resistance groups. The more unified our efforts, the stronger our impact will be."

Marcus, meanwhile, was making arrangements for the logistics of their next operation. "We've identified several strategic targets that could help us further undermine the regime's control. We need to prioritize these and ensure we have the resources in place to execute the plan effectively."

John walked over to the map on the wall, studying the latest updates. "We've made progress, but we can't afford to become complacent. The Harbinger's grip on global affairs remains strong, and we need to be prepared for any countermeasures they might deploy."

As they discussed their strategy, John's phone buzzed with an urgent message from one of their informants. The message was brief but alarming—there were reports of a major offensive planned by the regime, aimed at crushing the burgeoning resistance and reasserting their dominance.

"This changes things," John said, showing the message to the team. "The regime is gearing up for a decisive strike. We need to act quickly to counter their plans and protect the resistance."

The team sprang into action, adjusting their plans to address the imminent threat. They coordinated with allied resistance groups and devised a multi-faceted strategy to both defend against the regime's offensive and continue their campaign against the Harbinger's operations.

As the days passed, the resistance prepared for the impending battle. Training intensified, resources were allocated, and alliances were solidified. The stakes were high, and everyone understood the gravity of the situation.

The day of the offensive arrived with a palpable tension in the air. John's team and their allies took their positions, ready to face the regime's forces. The clash was intense, with both sides engaging in fierce combat. The resistance fought valiantly, determined to protect their hard-won gains and secure a future free from tyranny.

The battle was hard-fought, but the resistance's efforts paid off. They managed to repel the regime's offensive, inflicting significant losses and buying crucial time for further operations. The victory was a testament to the resilience and bravery of those who had come together to fight for a better future.

As the dust settled from the battle, John and his team regrouped. They were exhausted but determined. The victory had bolstered their morale and reinforced their resolve. They knew that the struggle was far from over, but they had taken a significant step toward dismantling the regime's control and challenging the Harbinger's influence.

John addressed the team, his voice filled with conviction. "We've faced tremendous challenges, and we've emerged victorious. But the fight continues. The regime and the Harbinger will not surrender easily. We need to stay vigilant, adapt our strategies, and continue working toward a future where freedom and justice prevail."

The team nodded in agreement, their spirits lifted by the recent success. They knew that the path ahead would be difficult, but they were prepared to face the challenges with unwavering determination.

As the sun set, casting a warm glow over the landscape, John and his team looked toward the future with hope and resolve. The dawn of a new era was on the horizon, and they were at the forefront of the struggle to shape that future.

The chapter concluded with a sense of cautious optimism. The resistance had achieved a significant victory, but the fight was far from over. The team was ready to continue their battle against the Harbinger and the regime, knowing that their efforts were making a difference in the ongoing struggle for freedom and justice.

John Carter's team had spent the following weeks regrouping and reassessing their strategy in the wake of their hard-won victory. They had managed to fend off the regime's major offensive, but they knew that the Harbinger would regroup and plan its next move.

In the heart of their temporary command center, the team was engaged in a heated discussion. Marcus, who had been reviewing recent intelligence reports, spoke up. "The regime's offensive was a significant setback for them, but it's clear that they're not going to back down. We need to keep our momentum and exploit their vulnerabilities."

Clara nodded in agreement. "We've gained the support of several new resistance groups, but we need to coordinate our efforts to ensure we're not just a collection of independent cells. Unity is key if we're going to make a sustained impact."

Rachel was examining the latest communications from their allies. "We've received reports of increased surveillance and crackdowns in several regions. The regime is tightening its grip, trying to suppress any remaining pockets of resistance."

John, standing by the map on the wall, traced a line with his finger. "We need to focus on disrupting their supply chains and communication networks. If we can undermine their infrastructure, we can create openings for further operations and alleviate some of the pressure on our allies."

The team agreed and quickly set about implementing their new plan. They organized covert operations to target key regime assets, gather intelligence, and support their allies. Their actions ranged from sabotage missions to intelligence gathering and coordination with local resistance cells.

One night, as the team was preparing for a critical mission, John received an unexpected call from one of their informants. The voice on the other end was urgent and strained. "We have a situation. The Harbinger is planning a major summit with world leaders. They're positioning it as a peace conference, but it's likely a strategic move to consolidate power and legitimize their regime."

John's eyes narrowed. "We need to find out more about this summit. If the Harbinger is using it to bolster their control, it could be a crucial opportunity for us to expose their true intentions and rally more support for the resistance."

The team mobilized to gather intelligence on the summit. They infiltrated the event's security perimeter, blending in with the crowds and using their skills to gather information on the Harbinger's plans. The summit was heavily guarded, and access to the inner circles was tightly controlled, but the team managed to obtain critical details about the Harbinger's strategy.

At the summit, the Harbinger delivered a powerful speech, presenting a façade of peace and unity while subtly reinforcing their agenda of global control. The speech was met with a mixture of applause and skepticism from the attendees. John's team was able to capture footage of the Harbinger's rhetoric, exposing the underlying threats and manipulation hidden beneath the surface.

The footage was quickly disseminated to the public, sparking outrage and further unrest. The resistance used the information to rally support, exposing the regime's duplicity and encouraging more people to join their cause. The Harbinger's summit, intended to strengthen their position, had instead become a catalyst for increased resistance and global scrutiny.

As the team reviewed the aftermath of the summit, John addressed his team. "We've managed to turn the Harbinger's summit into a turning point for us. The exposure of their true agenda has galvanized support and increased pressure on their regime. But we can't afford to rest on our laurels. We need to capitalize on this momentum and continue pushing forward."

The team prepared for their next phase of operations, knowing that their struggle was far from over. They continued their efforts to undermine the regime's control, support their allies, and expose the Harbinger's plans. The battles ahead would be challenging, but they were driven by a renewed sense of purpose and determination.

As the chapter drew to a close, John and his team stood at the precipice of a new phase in their struggle. They had achieved significant victories, but the path forward remained fraught with danger. With the Harbinger's influence waning and resistance growing stronger, the stage was set for the next chapter in their fight for freedom and justice.

Epilogue: The New Dawn

The world was in turmoil, but amidst the chaos and destruction, a new sense of hope began to emerge. The resistance had succeeded in exposing the Harbinger's true nature and rallying widespread support. The regime's grip on global affairs had begun to weaken, and the tides of the struggle seemed to be shifting in favor of those fighting for freedom and truth.

John Carter stood on a hill overlooking what was once a city engulfed in darkness but now showed signs of renewal. The skyline was marked by makeshift shelters and community efforts to rebuild, while the remnants of the Harbinger's regime lay in tatters. The scars of the conflict were still visible, but there were also signs of resilience and determination.

He glanced at his team, gathered around him, their faces reflecting both exhaustion and optimism. Clara, Marcus, Rachel, and the others were discussing their next steps and planning how to consolidate the gains they had achieved. The camaraderie and resolve among them were palpable, and John felt a surge of pride for what they had accomplished together.

The communications from their allies were encouraging. Communities that had been silenced under the regime were beginning to speak out, and new alliances were forming to support the rebuilding process. The global response to the resistance's revelations had been overwhelmingly positive, and many were now working to establish systems of governance that honored freedom and justice.

John's thoughts turned to the future. The struggle was far from over; there were still battles to be fought and challenges to overcome. But the resistance had proven that the human spirit could withstand even the darkest of times and emerge stronger. They had shown that courage and unity could defy tyranny and reclaim hope.

As he walked through the makeshift camp, he was approached by Emily and their children, Sarah and David. Emily's eyes were filled with a mixture of relief and determination. "We've come so far," she said softly, taking John's hand. "But there's still so much work to be done."

John nodded, squeezing her hand reassuringly. "We've made a difference, but the real challenge now is to build a future that reflects the values we fought for. We need to ensure that the sacrifices made were not in vain."

The family embraced, finding solace in their togetherness and the promise of a better future. The resilience and hope they shared would be the foundation upon which they would build the new world emerging from the ashes of the old.

In the quiet moments that followed, John and his team reflected on their journey and the path ahead. They had witnessed the rise of a new dawn, one forged through struggle and sacrifice. They were ready to face whatever challenges lay ahead, knowing that their efforts had made a tangible impact.

As the sun set, casting a warm glow over the horizon, John looked out with a sense of cautious optimism. The new dawn was not just a metaphor for the end of darkness but a symbol of the enduring spirit of humanity. The road ahead would be long and arduous, but the lessons learned and the strength gained would guide them through the trials to come.

With renewed determination, John Carter and his team prepared to continue their fight for a just and free world. The struggle was far from over, but they faced it with hope, knowing that the future was theirs to shape.

As the days turned into weeks, the world continued its slow but steady recovery. The fall of the Harbinger had created a power vacuum, and the process of rebuilding was fraught with difficulties. Nations that had been under the regime's control were now grappling with the challenges of establishing new forms of governance and addressing the scars left by years of oppression.

John Carter and his team remained at the forefront of these efforts, working tirelessly to support the reconstruction and help guide the transition to a more equitable society. Their days were filled with meetings, negotiations, and coordination with various factions working to rebuild their communities. The team's expertise and experience were invaluable as they navigated the complexities of this new era.

Amidst the logistical challenges, the human element of their work became increasingly evident. Stories of personal triumphs, acts of bravery, and the rebuilding of communities began to emerge. John and his team found themselves at the heart of many of these stories, providing support and hope to those who needed it most.

One evening, as John reviewed reports in the command center, Clara entered with a hopeful smile. "We've made significant progress," she said, holding up a newly signed agreement. "The first steps toward international cooperation are in place. Several nations have committed to working together to ensure a stable and just future."

John glanced at the document, his expression reflecting both satisfaction and concern. "It's a start. But there's still a long way to go. The challenges we face are immense, and the transition will be difficult. We must remain vigilant and committed."

Rachel, who had been working on humanitarian efforts, joined them. "We're seeing positive changes on the ground as well. People are coming together to rebuild their lives and communities. The resilience and spirit of the human race are truly remarkable."

John nodded. "It is. The sacrifices we've made have paved the way for a brighter future, but it's crucial that we continue to work together and address the ongoing issues. The world's healing is a process, not an event."

The team spent the following days traveling to various regions affected by the conflict, offering assistance and gathering firsthand accounts of the rebuilding efforts. They witnessed the emergence of new leaders, the growth of grassroots movements, and the gradual return of normalcy to once-devastated areas.

In one poignant moment, John visited a newly constructed community center where people were celebrating the reopening of their local gathering place. As he spoke with residents, he was struck by their determination and optimism. They shared stories of how their communities had come together during the darkest times and how they were now looking forward to a future built on cooperation and mutual support.

The center's walls were adorned with murals depicting scenes of unity and hope, a testament to the enduring spirit of those who had endured and overcome the regime's darkness. John felt a profound sense of fulfillment as he realized that their struggle had not been in vain. The seeds of change they had planted were beginning to bear fruit.

As the sun set on another day of rebuilding, John and his team gathered for a moment of reflection. They stood together on a hill overlooking a city that was slowly coming back to life. The sky was painted with hues of orange and pink, a symbolic reminder of the new beginning they had all fought for.

John addressed his team, his voice filled with gratitude and resolve. "We've come a long way, and our journey is far from over. The world we fought for is taking shape, and every step we take brings us closer to a future of hope and justice. Let's continue to work together, support each other, and keep moving forward."

The team nodded in agreement, their faces reflecting a renewed sense of purpose. The road ahead would be challenging, but they were ready to face it with the same courage and determination that had carried them through the darkest times.

As the weeks progressed, John Carter and his team worked tirelessly to help shape the new world emerging from the remnants of chaos. The once fractured global landscape began to show signs of unity and recovery. International summits were held, and collaborative efforts aimed at rebuilding infrastructure, restoring economies, and fostering international cooperation became the focus of their endeavors.

John's role as a leader extended beyond tactical decisions; he became a symbol of hope and perseverance. His days were filled with visits to various regions, where he would speak with local leaders, offer encouragement, and oversee the implementation of rebuilding programs. He found inspiration in the strength and resilience of the people he encountered, who were working hard to reconstruct their lives and communities.

In one such visit to a rural area, John met with a group of young volunteers who had organized a community garden to help address food shortages. The sight of young people coming together to create something positive out of adversity was a powerful reminder of the world's potential for renewal.

Back at the command center, Emily and the children were busy with their own contributions. Emily had taken on a key role in coordinating humanitarian aid, while Sarah and David participated in educational programs designed to teach skills for the new world. The family's dedication to rebuilding was evident in their every action, and their presence was a source of strength and comfort to John.

The resistance's efforts had also led to the establishment of several new initiatives aimed at addressing the underlying issues that had contributed to the rise of the Harbinger's regime. There were programs focused on education, healthcare, and the promotion of ethical governance. These initiatives sought to create a more just and equitable society and to prevent the rise of future threats.

One evening, as John reviewed progress reports, he received a message from an old friend, Marcus. The message was brief but hopeful: "We've made significant strides. There are still challenges ahead, but the spirit of collaboration and hope is stronger than ever. The future is looking brighter."

John smiled at the message, feeling a deep sense of accomplishment and hope. The challenges of rebuilding were far from over, but the progress made so far was a testament to the power of collective effort and resilience. He knew that the road ahead would be filled with obstacles, but the strength of the global community and the lessons learned from their struggle would guide them through.

As the sun dipped below the horizon, John took a moment to reflect on the journey that had brought them to this point. The world was far from perfect, but the progress made since the fall of the Harbinger was a sign that positive change was possible. The new dawn they had fought for was beginning to take shape, and it was up to them to nurture and protect it.

Gathering his team, John addressed them one final time. "We've come so far, and we've achieved so much. The future we fought for is within reach, but it's our responsibility to ensure that we continue to build on the progress we've made. Let's stay vigilant, stay hopeful, and keep working together to create a world that reflects our highest ideals."

The team nodded in agreement, their faces reflecting a shared commitment to the cause. As they prepared to embark on the next phase of their journey, John felt a renewed sense of purpose. The struggle had been arduous, but the promise of a better future made every sacrifice worthwhile.

With the world beginning to heal and the foundation of a new era being laid, John Carter and his team faced the future with a sense of hope and determination. The story of their struggle and triumph would continue to inspire future generations, serving as a reminder of the enduring strength of the human spirit and the power of collective action.

As the stars emerged in the night sky, John looked out over the city that was slowly being rebuilt, knowing that the dawn of a new era had arrived. The legacy of their fight would endure, and the promise of a brighter future lay ahead. The world was poised for a new beginning, and John Carter and his team were ready to face whatever challenges came their way, with hope lighting their path forward.

Publisher & Author:
B. A. Harris Publishing's
Email: b.a.harris.publishings@gmail.com
First Edition: August 16, 2024

DEAR READER,

Thank you for choosing to read Ending the Old: Ascension Day. Your support and interest mean a great deal to us at B. A. Harris Publishing's.

We invite you to explore our website for this book and many others at the website below.

Your engagement and feedback are invaluable to us as we continue to offer content that aims to enlighten and inspire. Thank you once again for your readership and support.

Sincerely,

B. A. Harris

B. A. Harris Publishing's

Don't miss out!

Visit the website below and you can sign up to receive emails whenever B. A. Harris publishes a new book. There's no charge and no obligation.

https://books2read.com/r/B-A-ZISSB-KLTSE

BOOKS 2 READ

Connecting independent readers to independent writers.